SHADOWS

AMONG THE

RUINS

SHADOWS

AMONG THE

RUINS

MARIE ROMERO CASH

Seattle, WA

Published by Camel Press

PO Box 70515

Seattle, WA 98127

Cover photograph by David Alfaya
Cover design by Sabrina Sun

Contact: info@camelpress.com

Copyright © 2011 by Marie Romero Cash

ISBN: 978-1-60381-834-6 (Paper)
ISBN: 978-1-60381-835-3 (Cloth)
ISBN: 978-1-60381-836-0 (ePub)

Dedication

For Jimmy:

I hear angel wings flutter when I speak your name

Acknowledgments

I would like to thank my brother, Ricardo, for providing such great material for my stories (you prove that life makes for good fiction); my brother-in-law Jean, who contributed tales about Idaho and law enforcement; Forrest Fenn, who, many years ago, let me introduce him to the San Lazaro Indian ruins; and for Gregory, Audrey and Anthony, the Lomayesva clan, for encouraging me to keep writing.

Prologue

Jemimah Hodge first ran into Tim McCabe at the glitzy Buckaroo Ball in Santa Fe. He was schmoozing at the bar with Byron Mills, a jerk she recognized from her past. She stopped dead in her tracks, disconcerted that she even remembered the lecherous old man. She had no intention of giving him the pleasure of knowing that.

Byron strutted toward her, an apish grin on his face. "What's a nice Mormon girl like you doing out here in this godforsaken desert?"

She gave him a phony smile and tossed her ponytail as if it belonged to her prized horse. She wanted to tell the son of a bitch to go to hell. Instead she picked her words carefully.

"That's *Doctor* Mormon Girl. And I hope you never need avail yourself of my services."

"Whoops," Byron responded, his drink sloshing on the hardwoods when he almost collided with another patron of the bar. "Folks, we have a gen-u-ine professional person here. What are the services you might offer?"

"I'm an inspector of dead bodies. You got any skeletons in your closet?"

Byron made a lavish fake bow and announced: "Whoops, folks, this lovely lady is a cor-oh-nerrh."

"No, you jerk. *Not* a coroner." She hated that word. "A forensic psychologist. I profile perverts and sadistic killers."

Byron preened. "Well, that lets me off."

Still at the bar, Jem caught McCabe's eyes on her and Byron. She shot him a 'rescue me' glance. McCabe excused himself from his drinking buddies and ambled over. She'd met McCabe once before but couldn't remember where, probably at the feed store. All she knew right now was that she needed someone to interrupt Byron's arrogant confrontation. And he wasn't going away without encouragement.

"Move aside, Byron, and give a real man a chance. My wife said I could dance with the second prettiest woman in the room and this one definitely qualifies." He reached out to Jemimah.

She took his hand. "Gladly."

1

Walking her horse up the arroyo, Jemimah Hodge heard a shot, the third one in the last half hour. As soon as she reached flat ground, she mounted her Appaloosa, keeping her feet hard in the stirrups as the horse loped along the fence toward the San Lazaro pueblo ruins. She had already worked up a sweat, and the morning breezes were cool on her overheated skin. She kept an eye out for a running spring to water her thirsty horse.

Ahead, she saw McCabe's shiny silver Hummer.

Near Medicine Rock, a pile of clothes lay on the shale, as if someone was in a hurry to shuffle out of them. There was no pool around to dive into, and running naked in the broiling sun was not a good way to escape the heat.

No, that was not just a pile of clothes. There was a body inside. And although the face was turned away, she was pretty sure she recognized McCabe's frame.

A noisy jaybird in a mesquite tree brought Jemimah to a halt. Dismounting her horse, she looped the reins over a fence post and hurried toward the ruins. She knelt and placed her fingers on his neck. A faint pulse. What could she do? She wasn't any good at mouth-to-mouth. Don't panic, stay calm, she whispered to herself.

Her cell phone was still plugged into the battery back at the ranch. She checked McCabe's pockets. Nothing. Her heart raced as she sprinted toward his vehicle. Maybe his cell phone was in the Hummer. And hopefully it would pick up a signal. Cellular service out here in the boondocks was sporadic at best.

She yanked open the Hummer door, eyeing the seat, the floorboard, the sun visors, before she spotted the phone on the dashboard next to the radio. She breathed deeply to steady her shaking hands and pressed 911 into the keypad.

"Come on, dammit," she muttered. "Answer!"

The operator came on the line. "What is your emergency?"

Jemimah practically screamed into the cell. "There's a guy here on the ground and he seems to be dying—" God, what a screw-up she was. Calm down, Jem.

"Where is here?"

"Just south of Cerrillos, next to the Indian ruins at the end of 55A—"

"Is he breathing?"

"He's not moving. He may have been shot."

"Ma'am, is he breathing? Do you know how to take his pulse?"

"Can you send someone in a hurry? Maybe a helicopter? He's not going to last much longer."

"Look. Calm down. Can you tell me if he is breathing?"

"Yes. I took his pulse. It's weak, but fast. Tachycardia, I think."

"Are you a doctor, ma'am?"

"Not an MD, no, but my training is clinical psychology. I've taken a number of First Aid courses but I've forgotten some of them."

"I'm contacting an officer right now."

"Listen, I need to get back to McCabe right now and see if I can help him."

"Just a couple more questions. What is your name and can you remain there until we send help?"

"Yes, of course. And my name is Jem—that's jay, ee, em—Hodge. I own the Peach Springs Ranch at the base of the Ortiz Mountains." She didn't add, '… and a border collie named Molly, a long-haired tabby cat named Gato' or that there was a barn for her two horses.

"Lieutenant Romero is in the vicinity of the Corrections Facility. He's on his way. Give him twenty minutes. Ambulance also on the way."

Jemimah punched off the cell phone and stashed it in her pocket. She rifled through McCabe's Hummer, grabbed a blanket and a First Aid Kit, and ran back to his side to check his pulse again. Fearing she would make his injuries worse, she debated then decided against turning him on his back. Then she changed her mind and gently eased him flat on the rock, rolling up the blanket and putting it under his head for a pillow. He moaned and tried to lift his head.

"Take it easy, McCabe." She gently stroked his brow. "You've been shot, but I don't think it's a critical wound. Just hang in there. Help is coming."

McCabe mumbled something unintelligible.

"Yes, yes," she soothed. "The ambulance is on the way. Don't try to talk. I'm right here."

Unbuttoning his shirt, she applied a handful of gauze pads to the wound. The bleeding seemed to have stopped. Not knowing what else to do, she stroked his temples and held fast to one hand. Once, he opened his eyes and gave her a forlorn look before passing out again. Damn, she hated being so helpless.

She looked down the road, hoping to see the rising cloud of dust that would mean help had arrived. Nothing. She turned her attention back to McCabe. His face was drained of color. He had lost a lot of blood. She wondered again about giving him mouth-to-mouth but suspected his lungs might be too messed up to receive it. A tinge of fear shot through her as she looked around the ruins. The shooter could still be out there.

2

Sheriff's Deputy Lieutenant Rick Romero drove south on Highway 14, lights flashing and siren blaring. A blue and white ambulance tailed him. A Santa Fe native, Romero had worked as a detective for the Sheriff's Office for the past fifteen years, slowly moving up to his rank as Lieutenant.

In his early forties, Romero's muscular physique resulted from working out regularly at The Body Factory, across from the National Cemetery in Santa Fe. With his brown hair and green eyes, he scarcely resembled a stereotypical Hispano of northern New Mexico, frequently referred to as beaners, La Raza, and sometimes spicks.

Over a year ago the Santa Fe County Commission approved the installation of a substation for the Sheriff's Department in the town of Cerrillos, about twenty miles south of Santa Fe. A day seldom passed without emergency calls about domestic disturbances, local merchants apprehending shoplifters, or a pack of coyotes camped out in front of the church. The new office prevented deputies from driving twenty miles from Santa Fe to investigate minor complaints.

The powers that be selected Detective Rick Romero to manage the satellite, not only because of his stature in the department, but because he was the single individual the Sheriff most trusted, regardless of the fact that his brother was locked up in the adult corrections facility across the street from the Sheriff's Department. In spite of other personal shortcomings, Romero was a trained forensic specialist with the ability to follow a crime investigation through to the end. His relentlessness had pitched him into hot water more than once in his career.

Romero was headed back to his office in Cerrillos when he received the call about the shooting. Often the site of drug busts, carjackings, and marital disputes, Cerrillos was an area he knew like the contours of his face. The small village had a colorful history from the mining boom in the late 1800s. The nearby mountains had long been considered a prime source of blue-green turquoise. The newly designated substation and increased police surveillance was a welcome addition to many of the residents, but not all. Drug dealers and users now had to watch their backs.

The elementary school on Highway 14 had just dismissed classes for the year, and parents' cars were streaming in a long line from the school drive onto the highway. Romero knew that drivers tended to ignore police vehicles, acting as though hypnotized by the flashing lights, so he cranked up the siren even louder to warn them to pull over to the side of the road. Police and emergency vehicles could only travel ten MPH above the speed limit. He was clocking seventy on the flat stretch of road. The ambulance had picked up on his tail and ran close behind him, sirens screeching in tandem. He took a left turn onto the county road. His cruiser fishtailed violently as the tires caught the pitted, washboard road. He knew it would be impossible to drive at a speed faster than twenty, so he slowed down until he turned at the railroad trestle, where he found the roads weren't much better. Under normal circumstances, this would have been a leisurely drive. He had never been this far off-road. Didn't even know anything existed past the turnoff.

The dirt road continued for another five miles, rocks spattering the underside of his vehicle. Traveling faster was still not an option. Up ahead the road forked, splitting the county road into two. A bright blue sign on top of a metal post read Crawford Ranch Road and directed him to take a right turn. He drove another three miles until he saw the ranch house and the Indian ruins.

Jemimah checked her watch. Thirty-five minutes had elapsed since she made the first call. Still no sign of a vehicle. She focused on McCabe, checking his pulse frequently, terrified each time that there would be none. Breathing still and shallow. Hadn't made another sound.

Finally, a siren wailed in the distance, drawing closer. The silver Santa Fe County Sheriff's SUV pulled into the side road, drove through the gate and came to a screeching halt. Lieutenant Romero stepped out of his vehicle and hurried over to Jemimah. "What's going on here, Ma'am?"

She pointed to the injured man lying motionless about ten feet away. "Over there. Looks like he's hurt pretty bad."

The ambulance ground to a stop behind the SUV. Two EMTs jumped out, one with a stethoscope around his neck. The other ran to the back of the ambulance to grab the gurney and eased it down the rocky drive. One of them slapped an oxygen mask over McCabe's mouth and placed the canister next to him. He listened for a heartbeat while the other started an IV, balancing it precariously on its stand, and then applied bandages around the wound. The EMTs lifted the injured man onto the gurney, placed the paraphernalia on the side and wheeled him over the rocky driveway to the back of the ambulance. The EMT slammed the door shut and the vehicle headed back toward Santa Fe, leaving a trail of thick dust. Romero walked over to Jemimah and pulled a small notebook out of his back pocket.

"Sorry to take so long introducing myself. First things first. I'm Lieutenant Rick Romero of the Santa Fe County Sheriff's office," he said. "McCabe's a lucky man you were in the vicinity. I need to ask you a few questions and then get over to the hospital to see how he's doing."

"All right," Jemimah said. "I think I've stopped shaking enough now to answer coherently."

"Tell me what you saw. Any particular reason you were in the area?" Romero asked.

"I was riding along the fence looking for a way to go back to my place without cutting all the way across over to Galisteo. I live a short walk south of here—near those mountains. I didn't realize everything was fenced off. I was just coming around the hill there when I heard a shot. I heard one earlier, too," Jemimah said.

"Do you know Mr. McCabe?" he said.

"Acquainted, that's all. Met him at a fundraiser in Santa Fe a few months ago." Jemimah handed him her card. "You can reach me at this number most days."

Romero glanced at the card before putting it in his Dayminder. Jemimah Hodge, PhD, Forensic Psychologist. On the back of the card it read: *Exploring the Criminal Mind.*

Jemimah told him how she discovered McCabe in front of the cave. "I figured it was just somebody out shooting at beer cans."

"Okay, Mrs. Hodge ..."

"Miss."

"Miss Hodge. Just what is a forensic psychologist?" He asked with a half-smile, thinking, *another Anglo woman moving to the southwest to launch a career ... probably from California.*

"I profile perverted, sadistic killers. Know any?"

"Not at the moment—at least, I hope not. And here's my card. If you think of anything else pertaining to this situation, I'd appreciate a call." Romero said.

Jemimah mounted her horse.

"Oh," and Romero added, "I will be in touch in a couple of days."

He lingered a bit longer than necessary. She had a feeling he was about to ask her for a date. As she rode through the gate, she could feel his eyes on her, evidently watching her hips move in rhythm with the horse's gait. Jem wondered if there was a single man in this so-called Land of Enchantment who didn't have anything other than sex on his mind.

3

St. Vincent's Hospital, or as locals referred to it, St. Victim's, was just off the interstate on St. Michael's Drive. The only hospital in this city of sixty-thousand inhabitants, the facility had been in existence since the mid 1860s. Several times large Albuquerque hospitals attempted to provide services in this community, but the Board of Directors of St. Vincent's fought them. The single hospital continued to monopolize health care for the citizens of Santa Fe, heedless of the complaints about long waits and lack of beds.

Dr. Amos Hillyer, chief surgeon at the hospital, came out of the scrub room, walked into Room 3 of the surgical ward, and leaned over the patient on the table being prepped for surgery.

"McCabe, what are you doing here?"

McCabe grunted, words indistinguishable.

"Found any decent relics lately?"

Another grunt.

"You can hear me, can't you?" the surgeon asked.

"Yes," whispered McCabe.

"Are you having trouble breathing?"

"Some."

"Are you in pain?"

"Chest."

"You know you were shot about an hour ago?"

"Hurts."

"Is your family around?"

"Wife. Home."

"We need to call her, get her over here."

McCabe whispered the number. "Two … nine … four …" His voice trailed off.

"Never mind. We can get it from information. Right now you're going to into the OR. We're going to patch you up."

The anesthesiologist fastened the blood pressure cuff around McCabe's arm and pumped it up. When it shut off, he glanced at the doctor. "200 over 140. I think you'd better let Oldham take over."

To Hillyer the anesthesiologist looked like he still belonged in high school. Panic was written all over his face. He wasn't going to be able to handle the pressure. "Get Oldham." Hillyer turned back to McCabe.

"Won't be but a minute or two. Hang in there. Were you digging in the ruins when you were shot?"

"Uhmmm."

"Probably some gold buried there."

"Not."

"Did you see who shot you?"

"Uh-hunh."

* * *

Romero wound his way through the hospital entry, which might have been the set of a television soap opera. An orderly directed him to a woman who stood at a long oval counter, shuffling papers and explaining to a patient that he could not leave until formally dismissed.

"Excuse me, Ma'am," Romero said.

"Sorry, you'll have to wait your turn."

Romero flashed his badge.

"Well, how was I to know?" she snapped. "You're not wearing a uniform. Is Tommy Hilfiger now on the Sheriff's payroll? Talk to that woman over there." She pointed to the nurse making notes on the patient board.

The nurse's name tag identified her as Priscilla Garcia, RN. He approached her, badge in hand.

"How can I help you?"

"Estoy buscando un paciente—"

"Don't you speak English?"

Romero blushed in irritation. Seemed like nobody spoke Spanish anymore, or were too embarrassed. "I'm looking for a patient brought into the ER within the last hour. Bullet wound in his chest."

"Could that be Timothy McCabe? I believe he's undergoing emergency surgery," she said, turning back to the board.

"Do you know if his family has been notified?" Romero asked.

"We're checking records for a phone number." She pointed toward a room at the end of the hallway. "You can wait there, Officer. Help yourself to the coffee."

"Thank you. I'd appreciate it if you'd keep me posted."

Romero checked his cell phone and sat down in the waiting room. He had missed a number of calls. He returned the most recent, figuring the earlier ones were no longer important. Two hours later the nurse came to find him, a grim look on her face.

4

Laura McCabe paced the floor between her den and the kitchen of their Santa Fe home. She was far too anal retentive, but she could not stand it when Tim deviated from a tight schedule, involving himself in his damned ruins and losing all sense of time.

Where in Heaven's name was he and why hadn't he called? The cat was clawing the Navajo rugs on the floor in the living room and had its eye on the woven red and black Chief's Blanket that hung on the wall. The silly thing had been known to scale right up the blanket in chase of a gecko lizard. She screamed, "Tiger, stop that!" but of course it paid her no attention. She shook her turquoise bracelets at Tiger, which usually irritated him and caused him to run under the bed. Not this time.

She stopped at the nineteenth century wooden Santo on the long Parsons table in the hall and ran her fingers over the polychromed carving. Her cleaning woman, Rosa, swore by these saints, claiming they calmed her nerves. She would whisper, "Calma me, Dios, Calm me, God," as she walked around the house with a feather duster in her hand. The saints offered little comfort to Laura.

Late again. Up to his neck in dust. Totally unaware of the time of the day. Now she needed to call her friends and arrange to meet at La Fonda for cocktails instead of sending the limo driver to pick them up.

Perhaps Tim had run into a fellow dealer and purchased something that he needed to carry to the gallery. God knows their three-car garage was already full of relics. She drove the six blocks to Canyon Road and parked at the side of the building. As usual, Canyon Road bustled with tourists wandering in and out of the gift shops, galleries and clothing boutiques. At Wind Medicine, the gallery lights were off;

they did not stay open late, preferring in general to work by appointment.

Laura entered through the side door. She reached to press the alarm code into the keypad then realized it hadn't gone on when she unlocked the door. That was odd.

Daylight streamed through the skylights, although dusk was only minutes away. She flipped the light switch in Tim's office and glanced at the desk calendar. Nothing to indicate that he would be anywhere but digging at the ruins. What the hell could be the reason for his delay? Her annoyance escalated. It wasn't like Tim to blow off something this socially important.

She decided she might as well make herself useful by going over the inventory sheets as she waited for his call on her cell. She heard a loud thump in one of the back rooms. It wasn't unusual for birds to fly into the glass windows; there were so many around this year, snowbirds from somewhere up north, like turistas.

Laura gave an approving look at the rows and rows of intricately painted Acoma Indian pottery they had gathered through the first ten years of their marriage. By the time they opened a gallery on Canyon Road near the historic plaza in Santa Fe, their reputation as knowledgeable dealers had grown. She was eternally grateful McCabe had never returned to law enforcement, although she knew he loved the challenge of solving a crime. Last month the Sheriff had dropped in unannounced to seek his advice. McCabe was in his element around law officers. He was never going to outgrow that.

She kept glancing at her watch as she made her way around the gallery. The minutes continued to tick away. Over an hour had passed. Still no call. By force of habit she checked her cell phone, just in case she had missed his call. Nothing. Well, at least she made some headway on the annual inventory. She walked back and placed it on the bookkeeper's desk. That would be one less task she would have to do next week. Rummaging for her keys, she heard someone trying the door, and then another thump. "Who could that be," she wondered. "The gallery's been closed since last weekend."

Laura started to reach for the doorknob, but changed her mind as someone started shoving on the door, trying to push it in. She ran over to the alarm module, punched the code in and set it off just as the door flew off its hinges. She screamed.

5

Many afternoons, long before McCabe came to San Lazaro, Charlie Cooper had roamed the Indian ruins with his .22 rifle in hand. In the summertime, he restricted himself to the shade of Medicine Rock, digging for Indian relics he could sell. Nothing so major he'd have to explain where it came from. Usually beads and bones he strung into necklaces and passed off as antiquities. This kept him in nachos and Dos Equis.

A few days after McCabe was shot, Charlie heard the putt-putt-putt noise of an old Ford pickup rambling toward the ruins. He wondered who'd come this late in the day. Couldn't be McCabe—he was probably still down for the count.

Someone shouted "Hello up there!" and strolled toward the gate. It was that son of a bitch Bart Wolfe, a short seedy-looking guy who hung out at the Mine Shaft Tavern, a few miles up the road from Cerrillos. Bart schlepped around in boot-cut jeans, engineer boots and a dirty white Grateful Dead T-shirt. A crumpled pack of Camels stuck out of his pocket. Keys dangled from a chain fastened to his belt loop.

Charlie had caught Bart powwowing at the bar with an exotic dancer named Linda, no mean piece of meat. That was a month ago and shortly thereafter, Charlie staked his own claim on the juicy Miss Starlight.

Charlie glanced at his .22 and decided it was more of a toy than a threat. Under the circumstances, he intended to play it cool. "Hey old man, how they hanging?"

The sun was directly behind Charlie, forcing Bart to shield his eyes with his hand. "Who is it?" Bart ambled to within a few feet of Charlie. "Oh. You."

Charlie poked a finger in Bart's chest and what came out of his mouth was not so cool. "You asshole. What the hell are you doing out here? You're trespassing on private property."

Bart did not seem greatly perturbed. "Hell, I was making my way over to the ranch to see you. I'm looking for Linda. Ain't seen her since that night in Madrid you carried her off."

"Can't help you, man." Charlie laughed a dirty snort. "Woman's like a Vegas poker chip going from hand to hand. Went from me to a guy in the parking lot the next time I took her out for a drink. Never even made him buy her a Coke."

Bart was floating like a feather in a dust bunny. High on something, Charlie thought. Another good poke and the son-of-a-gun would go flat on the ground.

"Like to see for myself," Bart said. "Mind if I go over to your house and check it out?"

"You calling me a liar? I told you Linda isn't there. Besides, I'm busy. Get the fuck on back to your own place."

"Ain't no call to be so nasty."

Charlie turned to walk away, but Bart grabbed his sleeve and pulled him off balance. "Come on, man. I gotta find her. She's my woman."

Charlie backed away. "Watch it, man. Don't finger the merchandise."

"Oh, you lookin' to get into a little fracas?" Bart asked.

"I ain't done nothing to you, but if you want to rumble, I'm always ready. He pulled out a knife and lunged at Charlie.

Without thinking, Charlie hefted his rifle to keep Bart away. Bart grabbed the bore, stumbled back, and tripped on his own boots. The gun went off. The first shot hit Bart and the second shot barely missed a cow that stood by the fence enjoying a salt lick.

Bart looked like he was about to throw up before he collapsed.

"Oh, shit," Charlie said.

Thinking Bart was dead, Charlie gathered his stuff and headed lickety-split toward the ranch. He kept repeating to himself, "It was an accident. It was an accident."

An hour later, Bart picked himself up and started up the road in his noisy truck. He made it about five miles and then pulled over to the side of the road. Bleeding profusely from his right arm, he crawled out of his truck, stood upright for a moment, then crawled back in and passed out over the steering wheel.

A rancher herding a couple of cows saw him slumped over, the horn blaring, and punched numbers in his cell for an ambulance.

6

On Wednesday of that week, Jemimah concluded her meeting with the personnel department. Hired as a forensic investigator for the Santa Fe County Sheriff's Department, she would spend much of her time not only working cases assigned to the main office but the Cerrillos substation as well. Her duties included profiling, conducting interviews, assisting in active investigations and resurrecting cold cases. Her skills on the shooting range needed to be honed. And after the fiasco with Tim McCabe, she decided to audit classes on CPR. The sheriff suggested she include seminars on police procedures and crime scene protocol.

As she strolled out of the complex toward her vehicle, Lieutenant Romero tapped his horn. She looked up and frowned. Keeping tabs on her again? He drove up next to her, reached over and pushed open the passenger door of his SUV.

"Hop in," he said. "I've been wanting to buy you lunch to celebrate your new appointment."

"Sorry, Rick, my day is filled with meetings and interviews. I'm trying to put together another forensic seminar, this time in Albuquerque."

"Oh for god's sake, Jem," he said with exasperation. "You have to eat somewhere sometime. There's a great new place just opened up on Alameda Road. I think it's early enough we can beat the lunch crowd."

"All right, you sold me." Jemimah smiled, climbed into the passenger seat, and clipped the seat belt on. "I only had coffee for breakfast." Who was she trying to convince? Herself or him?

Rick parked next to the curb in front of the building, got out and opened her door. The restaurant was busy, but they were seated quickly. The hostess led them to a corner booth.

"This is nice," Jemimah said.

Hanging from the ceiling were colorfully painted bicycle wheels of various sizes. She was looking up at them trying to make the connection.

"The name of the place is Xyclo. They specialize in Vietnamese cooking. The name refers to the three wheeled bicycles used to transport passengers around Asian cities," Romero said.

"Interesting," she said.

"I'm glad we have this chance to catch up. I've wanted to ask you out to dinner."

"Out, as in *date*?"

He smiled. "Yeah, something like that."

"Does the hierarchy frown on inter-departmental dating? I haven't read the five-hundred page employee handbook."

"Only with subordinates," he said. "I think we're on an equal plane here."

"I'll take that as a compliment," she said.

"Is that a yes?"

"No, it's a no. I think we're treading water, Lieutenant. I'm still annoyed with you for—"

"For what? My persistence in wanting you?"

"Among other things." She waved away the waiter who had come to take their order.

"What other things? That I might just treat you like a woman for a change?"

"More like a sex object. I don't appreciate going around town with you sporting me like a trophy."

"Sounds like you're a bit caught up in yourself, Doctor."

"Give me a call when you grow up to be a big boy. Anyway, Lieutenant Rick. Thanks for lunch." She tossed her napkin on the table and headed for the door. Romero motioned the waiter to bring him a drink.

7

The anonymous shooting of Tim McCabe caused most Santa Feans, who had no tolerance for crime, to stop buying the daily newspaper and watch sitcom reruns rather than expose themselves to the daily news, burying their heads in the sand like the proverbial ostrich. Others, like Anna Mali, slept with the lights on in every room.

Anna lived in a small apartment in the center of the historic Guadalupe District, a pre-1700s area of Santa Fe next to the equally old Our Lady of Guadalupe Church. Each time she heard a strange sound, she ran to the heavily curtained windows to peer out at the street. She was not averse to calling the cops if a wino set up shop on or near her doorstep. If a stranger knocked on her door, he was apt to stand there until accosted by the local federales. The cops who patrolled the Guadalupe beat nicknamed her Anxious Anna.

Anna wheeled a grocery basket to the checkout counter behind a tall, thirty-something guy purchasing cigarettes. She could not help but notice that he gave her an interested eye, and preened a little. She knew she was pretty. A little on the chubby side, but pretty nonetheless.

Her blond hair was pulled back in a tightly woven French braid, and she wore a pair of faded, too-snug jeans. She enjoyed a little anonymous attention, frequently misinterpreted by the interested parties. If they dared approach, she usually turned her back.

Anna engaged in some paltry banter with the checker, swiped her card on the machine, punched in her PIN numbers, and retrieved two plastic bags from the edge of the counter.

As she walked past him, the guy deliberately bumped into her. He started to apologize. Her friendly eye turned hostile. She straightened her back and quick-stepped through the automatic doors.

He went back to his truck, climbed in, smoked a cigarette, and watched Anna make her way across the parking lot.

Instead of entering a vehicle, Anna walked the sidewalk along the mall perimeter. As she strolled up a slight incline, she looked toward the cemetery across the road, white gravestones lined up in neat rows as far as the eye could see. She made a mental note to take flowers to her stepfather's grave.

The stranger drove slowly out of the parking lot, watching as she lingered in front of a corner boutique. Moving to the intersection, Anna punched the Walk button. He trailed her as she walked by the Lotaburger and the tattoo parlor next door. The man in the car behind him honked loudly then sped off, sticking his hand out in an obscene gesture.

The stranger drove around the block.

Anna headed up the hill toward the big bronze statue of Our Lady of Guadalupe installed on the north grounds of the church. The cord from her I-Pod was plugged firmly into her ears, Los Lobos singing "Hotel California." She crossed the street, pushed the iron gate open, and stopped to retrieve her mail from the mailboxes against the porch wall.

The stranger parked his truck next to the curb, exited his vehicle and reached the gate as she stood on the porch and rifled through her knapsack for a ring of keys. Still plugged into her I-pod, she was oblivious to his presence behind her.

She opened the door to her house, picked up the bag of groceries and, before she could scream, he placed his big latex-gloved hand over her mouth and pushed her into the living room.

Two days later the 911 operator answered a call from Myra Mali, a distraught woman who said she hadn't heard from her daughter for several days. The call was relayed to a patrol officer, who recognized the address of Anxious Anna. A small woman in her fifties stood on the porch of the residence. Still in black flannel pajamas, she reeked of stale cigarette smoke and cheap perfume.

Myra Mali tossed her cigarette on the porch floor and scrunched it with her foot as the patrolmen approached.

"I've been knocking at the door for about an hour and there's been no answer," she said.

"What about her job, does she work somewhere?" he asked. The patrolman stepped back, as if overpowered by her scent.

Myra tried to look through the curtained front door. "Anna was off until a few days ago. She didn't show up yesterday and wasn't answering her cell."

"Could she have gone somewhere for a few days?"

"No, she doesn't drive. I don't think she has a lot of friends. Look, I'm really worried. She's not like other girls." Myra scrunched up her face to hold back tears. "She doesn't party or do drugs. Pretty much keeps to herself. It's not like her not to keep in touch."

The officer searched the windows and the front of the house for signs of forced entry. Finding none, he knocked loudly and then with little effort pushed the door open. There were obvious signs of a struggle. Groceries littered the floor near the hallway. Melted Haagen-Dazs dulce de leche ice cream trickled from an overturned tub across the dark walnut floor. The unmistakable, sweet odor of rotting flesh infiltrated the house.

Myra pushed past the officer, but he put up an arm to hold her back. She slumped to her knees, sobbing hysterically.

8

Captain Jeff Whitney, a twenty-year veteran of the New Mexico State Police, was exhilarated. He had just returned to Santa Fe from a four week vacation, where he had attended a forensics update. The lecturer for one seminar had been a hot gal named Jemimah Something, who seemed to get off on talking about perverts and sadistic killers. The other two weeks, while fishing the Florida Keys in a dollar-an-hour rent-a-boat, he tried not to think about her. Not much success—either with the fish or the forgetting.

Work was no siren call for him. He wasn't anxious to return, but on the other hand, there wasn't much that could spoil his day. He still enjoyed the relaxation of walking the beach and breathing in the salty, ocean air.

He had cleared his desk the day before he left, but it now overflowed with case files both new and old. A manila envelope from the Chief caught his eye—a long-closed cold case involving the accidental death of a police officer's wife, that officer being his partner of several years. The memo indicated that the coroner had ruled the cause of death as "auto accident." Nothing to indicate otherwise. The Chief attached a note telling him to contact Jemimah Hodge, the new forensics investigator for the County, who might be able to give him some insight into the case.

Whitney's mind traveled back to Florida. Nah, this couldn't be the same Jemimah. Too coincidental. He pulled her card out of his wallet and felt like dancing a jig. "I'll be damned."

He shoved everything on his desk to the side and reached for the phone. As he dialed her number, he rehearsed what he was going to say. After a few rings the County Operator intercepted and directed him to voicemail. Whitney left a message and got back to work. Naw, he'd just go on over there. You can never tell about that voice-mail stuff. Didn't mean she wasn't there. Just not in the mood to answer the phone.

* * *

Jemimah sat at her desk in a corner office at the end of a long corridor, coffee mug in one hand, phone in the other.

Whitney stood at the door and watched her. She was wearing a honey-colored shirt with a dark blue skirt. Her legs looked great. The shoes looked a little matronly but he figured she was required to dress like the detectives in the Sheriff's Department. She looked to be in her mid-twenties, but her professional status seemed to indicate otherwise. Didn't really matter that much. He wondered if she was single. He'd dated married women before, but he had learned early on to first make sure their husbands weren't on the force.

Jem pointed a finger at him. "Officer Whitney? Florida, right? You followed me all the way from the Sunshine State?"

"These are my stomping grounds, ma'am."

She gave her head that little twist that shook her ponytail in a delightful manner. For some reason, it made him picture her on a horse. Then he saw the photograph.

"I see you have a picture of an Appaloosa on your desk. Somehow I didn't figure you for a ranch woman."

"That's Mandy. A horse is a necessary evil in this god-forsaken country." She reached out to shake his hand. "Seminar on Internet sex offenders, right?"

"Yes, I found your talk really compelling." A bit of flattery would certainly do no harm. One should never miss an opportunity to flatter a pretty girl. You could never tell what it might lead to. "And please call me Jeff."

When she took his hand, she noticed how firm and warm his hands were. She gazed at him a moment longer than she intended. Oh shit, he was going to think she was desperate for a date. "Take a seat."

Whitney pulled a wooden folding-chair up to her desk and handed her the manila envelope he'd found on his desk earlier that morning.

"And this is what?"

"A cold case I could use your help on."

Oh great, Jem thought. Pulling out these old cases so he could get next to her. Well, she knew how to handle that kind of Casanova. All business-like. Stay cool. But still, he was on the handsome side.

"Coffee?"

He grinned. He didn't intend to, but something strange was quarterbacking his hormones. "Got any Kahlua?"

"Just ran out, but there's a lounge down the street," she answered back. "Let me see what you have."

She took a few minutes to review the file, asking questions as she did so. "Did you know the victim, Rosa Ilfeld?"

"Rose. Her husband was my partner. He was also the only suspect. Her family's pushing the Department to reopen the investigation."

"Hard to keep an open mind under those circumstances, I would imagine."

"Don't get me wrong, I had a great deal of respect for Captain Ilfeld—still do. Known him a lot of years. But he told several people she was suffering from a disease when she really wasn't. Nonetheless, I don't see anything in the file to indicate that it was anything but an accident. Don't know why the powers that be want to dredge this whole thing up again."

"It doesn't make sense to me," Jemimah said. "If he had access to a police cruiser, he would have taken her to the ER in that, lights flashing and all."

"He chose to take her Corvette instead. Nothing wrong with that," he said.

Jemimah had the distinct impression Whitney wasn't interested in pursuing any kind of investigation. Maybe he was just using this case as an excuse to come on to her. "Oh my god!" she said. "Did you realize it's already five o'clock? Can I take this file home with me?"

Whitney feigned a distraught look. "Sorry, but it's our only file and I don't want to be responsible for it out of my sight. You would not believe how easily notes and other evidence can disappear from a file.

Jemimah smiled. He looked damned cute when he was upset. "Listen, Whitney, how about I buy you a drink at Los Angelos. We can talk about the case some more."

He grinned. "I'd much rather listen to good stories about pervert criminals or sadistic killers. You think it's too early for dinner?"

Los Angelos was a trendy Mexican restaurant on a side road in downtown Santa Fe which catered mostly to attorneys and white collar workers from state offices and the District Courthouse nearby. The polished cherry wood bar was filled to capacity. They sat in a circular booth near the window.

The waitress brought their order, Jalapeno poppers and Margaritas, followed by the evening special. Whitney moved the yellow scratch pad and file folder over to make room for the steaming plates, half-listening to the server's admonishment about the dishes being too hot, don't touch. He was thinking about something other than fajitas covered with guacamole, beans, and grilled chicken that would certainly be hot to the touch. The sound of Jemimah's ringing cell phone brought him back. Most men would be embarrassed at having romantic thoughts about a woman he barely knew. Not Whitney. He considered himself quite a ladies' man and she was fair game.

Jemimah answered the phone and excused herself from the table. It was Lt. Rick Romero.

"Hey, where've you been? I've been calling your office. And why aren't you answering your cell?"

"I answered. What's your beef? I'm working a case right now." She almost added that he didn't sign her weekly paycheck, but held her tongue.

"At cocktail time? You looking to get a raise?"

"Actually no. Jeff Whitney, a State Policeman, brought over a case he wanted my advice on."

"Jeff Whitney? Jeez, girl. Watch yourself. This guy's bad news. He's got more girlfriends than a monkey has fleas."

"Hey, I'm a big girl now. I can take care of myself."

She hung up the phone, wondering who the hell Rick thought he was, checking up on her like that. Next he would want to hire on as chaperone.

9

Pre-summer temperatures around Santa Fe vacillated between warm days and cool nights along with clear, star-filled skies. Nowhere in the United States were the skies bluer or wider. The county was surrounded by high mountain ranges, flat mesas, and hills populated by rocky outcroppings—a painter's paradise, an artisan's treasure trove. Potters who traveled south down La Bajada Hill on I-25 toward Albuquerque and ventured just off the road could gather clay in various shades of color. Also along Highway 14, which runs parallel to I-25, but they had to look a little harder.

This was true Indian Country, shrouded in mystery. Several early Indian tribes settled in the foothills of the Ortiz Mountains near Cerrillos and Madrid, on the stretch of land encircled by the Galisteo Basin. Popular theory claims that the Anasazi cultures collapsed due to severe drought. Survivors migrated to the Rio Grande Valley and became assimilated into today's modern pueblos.

There were two primary pueblo ruins in this area, the smaller one, San Marcos and the larger, San Lazaro. San Lazaro Pueblo was about eighteen miles southeast of Santa Fe, sixty acres of rolling hills sprinkled with junipers and piñons. Spiny cholla cactus outcropped the surface of sandy hills.

The historic ruins of the Tano Indian pueblo nestled along the Del Chorro Creek, where the stream trickled along, minding its own business, perfectly capable of becoming a raging deluge during the monsoon season. At various junctures, the stream went underground. High canyon walls lined the perimeter for a short distance and the terrain flattened into gently rolling hills.

Sharing a common boundary with the San Lazaro Indian ruins, the Crawford Ranch lies hidden in the center of a small valley. At the top of the hill next to the entrance, a windmill stands sentry.

Known as the Turquoise Trail, the landscape along Highway 14 remained the same—adobe houses on several-acre plots, neighbors more than an arm's length from each other. An old feed store converted part of its building to house a popular restaurant, the San Marcos Café. Tourists and locals alike traveled more than ten miles from Santa Fe to eat a roast beef burrito smothered with red chili or a plate of biscuits and gravy. Outside, turkeys, albino peacocks and chickens spread their wings with ease and mingled with the overgrown tabby, who eyed them with great interest, waiting for his chance.

Charlie Cooper lived at the Crawford Ranch, adjoining McCabe's San Lazaro Indian ruins. Not cut out for ranch life and eager to return to the city, owner Gary Blake had dispensed with requesting references from Charlie, whose down-home country charm convinced Blake he was the one for the job. Charlie survived out there quite nicely. Not only did he receive a monthly check from Blake for caretaking, but his only expenses were food, beer and gasoline, not necessarily in that order. Charlie grew a hefty crop of marijuana, part of which he sold to the local druggies. The larger portion was sold to a contact in Albuquerque.

Every now and then, a pothead snooped around to see what he could steal. The ranch was surrounded by old Indian ruins, and these characters dug around to find something for a quick sale. Problem was, there was only one road in and one road out, and Charlie was always willing to give chase. Hell, he looked forward to it.

Old man Loomis at the general store in Cerrillos had a lot of relics on his shelves he knew came from the Crawford Ranch. He didn't care where things originated—he always underpaid. The back of the store was filled with items bought from the derelicts who hung around outside, smoking their foul-smelling roll-your-owns and coming inside to take a piss in the employees' bathroom. Loomis accommodated them. Otherwise they did their number outside in plain sight, which tended to discourage tourists who might be potential customers for his not-only-phony but overpriced goods.

Today, Charlie entered the unfinished basement on the sub-level of the house to begin harvesting his prized marijuana plants. The room had an earthen floor, perfect for a hidden garden. *My ticket out of this hell-hole*, he mused. Over the last six months he had stashed about $22,000 in hundred dollar bills. This next sale would serve to take him over his goal: fifty grand.

The room was a marijuana forest. The plants had reached their peak and the buds dried nicely. He spent a few hours pulling them all out and hanging them from hooks. The pungent pine-cone odor was unmistakable.

Charlie inspected each plant, almost amber in color. He spent two days trimming buds. Wearing plastic gloves, he cut each plant with care and spread the leaves out in paper grocery bags, which he carried over to the back of the barn and covered with hay. It would take at least a week for these to cure before he could form them into brick-sized portions, shrink-wrap and weigh them.

For the remainder of the week, Charlie dug up every telltale sign of his pot-growing venture, loaded it all up in black garbage bags and hauled them to the County Dump. Satisfied with what he had accomplished, he drove into Cerrillos and used the pay phone in front of the general store to call his contact.

10

Since taking the helm of the satellite office in Cerrillos, Rick Romero spent little time at home. Many nights he stretched out on the office couch, too exhausted to drive back to Santa Fe. Off-duty, he drove a dark green Subaru, a vehicle his nephew called a preppie wagon, favored by WASP couples to drive kids to soccer scrimmage. Maybe it didn't fit his persona, but Romero liked the car. He'd bought it at a police auction—low mileage and not a scratch on it.

Romero lived in the house where he grew up, a small two bedroom '30s adobe on a side street in the South Capitol district of Santa Fe, a mile from the downtown Plaza. In recent years, he'd gutted the interior and replaced plumbing and electrical. He did not disturb his mother's small shrine to El Santo Niño de Atocha, an image of the child Jesus dressed in pilgrim garb. When she was alive, she often prayed to the saint if Romero strayed off-track. He smiled as he recalled how often that became a necessity.

Romero wasn't particularly religious, though he had been brought up Catholic. The devastating effect crime had on families caused him to wonder what kind of God allowed such atrocities. He stopped attending church when a priest friend was arrested for an affair with a fifteen-year-old girl. Father John endeared himself to many Native American pueblos in northern New Mexico. He grew his black hair long and wore it in braids fastened with sterling silver feathers. Together he and Romero attended many of the pueblo feast day ceremonies.

Romero was part of the task force set up by the FBI to arrest the priest when he met the girl at a local restaurant. She was outfitted with a concealed tape recorder. Subsequently, several other teenage girls claimed the priest lured them into sexual liaisons. Romero was devastated to discover the dark side of Father John. Hell, he had played basketball and gone fishing with this guy. It was also a blow to his professional pride that he hadn't picked up on the priest's nefarious activities.

What an asshole, Romero thought. All that time he had hidden his smutty secrets. Last he heard, the priest was serving a long sentence in a California prison while the archdiocese settled—more correctly, tried to avoid settling—numerous lawsuits.

Nonetheless, in spite of his disillusionment, Romero bought a votive candle every week at Walgreen's and lit it at his mother's shrine. He didn't need a church to exercise his faith or to show his mother he loved her.

It was already nine o'clock in the morning. He stopped by Dunkin' Donuts and picked up a box of assorted donuts and sweet rolls. The Sheriff was coming to the Cerrillos substation for their monthly meeting. Romero drove the seventeen miles to the office, his mind on the McCabe case.

The ring of his cell phone startled him. It was Jemimah.

"Hey, you sound a little distracted; everything all right?" she asked.

"On my way to work. Meeting the boss in an hour to go over my cases. What's up?"

"Do you have time later today? I have some theories I wanted to run by you on a cold case I'm working on. Maybe you can give me fresh perspective."

"Fresh perspective? Why do you want my opinion? Is this about McCabe? Maybe you can give me fresh perspective."

"No, not McCabe. But I need to run this by someone with experience."

Sheesh, Rick thought. Is she coming on to me, now? This woman didn't seem to know what she wanted.

"Hey, Jem, listen. I don't have my appointment book with me. Let me call you later and we can figure something out." He wasn't in the mood to play twenty questions. He said goodbye and flipped the cell phone closed. He made the turn into the driveway, gathered his files, and walked in the door.

The reception area was sparsely furnished with two battle-scarred desks that had come out of a warehouse in Santa Fe, two equally scarred Captain's chairs, a phone, fax machine, two computers, and a coffeemaker. The coffeemaker was new, because he had personally picked it up at Wal-Mart. Three overflowing file cabinets sat in one corner, next to a small nicked-leather couch in the seating area. A jumble of cables dangled over the edge of a desk, uniting the office communication system in a tangle of knots. The walls were a dull army gray, the Sheriff's idea of a suitable decorating scheme. In Romero's office, there was little on the walls except framed certificates, various diplomas, and a retablo of San Miguel—the patron saint of detectives and law enforcement. It was painted by his sister who, before she married and moved to Arizona, was a local Santera of some renown and painter of religious icons. He felt badly for not keeping in closer touch and made a note to give her a call. She had never forgiven him for allowing their Aunt Rita to take her home after their mother died.

For the past ten years Romero had been a card-carrying member of Alcoholics Anonymous. His drinking escalated after his partner was killed in a motorcycle accident. Alcohol ruined his first marriage. By the time he went into treatment, it was too late to salvage what was left. Months and months of appointments with a therapist brought him to terms with his childhood, his culture, and his father's own weakness for alcohol. About a year ago, after staying sober for ten years, Romero had slowly started drinking beer and the occasional cocktail, just to take the edge off. *Better than Xanax,* he thought.

His social drinking was starting to worry him a bit. If he ever got into another relationship with a woman, he would tell her right up front about his struggle. His father lost the battle after years of drinking, and his mother died some years later, probably from a broken heart. Romero was well aware how alcohol had ruined their lives. He sighed as he remembered how dark those days had been.

The sound of his assistant's tapping on his door made him jump. Clarissa handed him a sheaf of papers and four new case files.

"Why, Detective Romero, I must say you have a special glow about you," she said. "And is that a new pair of Justin boots you're wearing?"

He had known Clarissa for the better part of ten years. A friend of his sister's, she'd worked for the Department since high school. A petite woman, she knew how to push buttons, and the detectives respected her. When she heard he was going to head the Cerrillos satellite office, she volunteered to get things set up. She was still with him.

"Well, my *newest* pair of boots," he said.

"Listen, sweetie. You've got that faraway look in your eyes. Don't think I've ever seen that. You meet someone special?"

"None of your business."

"Can't get her out of your mind, huh?"

"Yeah, but I don't want to talk about it."

"Professional woman, I would guess."

"Guess all you want."

"Divorced, three kids, makes twice what you do."

"No."

"No to which?"

"No kids."

"She's in law enforcement. Not supposed to date fellow employees."

"If you have to know, she's a shrink. Specializes in criminal behavior."

"Looking into your dating practices? Those could be pretty criminal."

"Oh for god's sake, Clarissa, can we forget my love life?"

"Well, I can, but I'm not sure about you. You're still carrying a torch for your first wife. What does that make, seven years?"

"I'm getting over it."

The phone rang.

Clarissa laughed. "Saved by the bell. That woman who discovered McCabe after he was shot, right? The one that the Sheriff hired a while back as a forensic specialist?"

"Yep, that's the one. Sexy, too, rides a horse like a real cowgirl."

"So, you asked her for a date?"

"Working on it."

"No guts. You gonna answer the phone?"

His meeting with the boss turned out to be the usual waste of time. They talked about the same-old same-old. He didn't have anything to report and was glad Sheriff Medrano didn't have time to grill him. Romero knew these meetings were the Sheriff's way of taking the heat off himself with the elected officials and the press, who took advantage of every opportunity they could find to nail him to the cross.

Some shitty day this had been. He was sulking about Jemimah treating him like dirt, blowing up over every little thing he said. Well, she would soon be history. Yeah, he would still have to work with her, but it would be strictly business. He was sick of trying to get something going.

And now, he was going over to McCabe's to try to pull a rabbit out of a hat. He hadn't accomplished much lately and the Sheriff was on his ass. McCabe was the Sheriff's friend, Jemimah's friend too. Damn, maybe he should have just gone out and had a few drinks, but he had already scheduled the appointment.

11

Just in case the owner decided to travel all the way from Atlanta and show up unexpectedly, Charlie methodically cleaned up the ranch premises, task by task. He shoveled a three-month supply of manure from the paddocks and hid the moldy hay he had purchased behind a couple of fresh bales. He made a note to gather up the few cattle that wandered around the fifteen hundred acres.

There was an old nag wandering about the barnyard, her main enterprise being the swatting of flies with her tail. He returned her to the paddock and dug the curry comb out from under the cat's litter box. He reminded himself to get her reshod. The second corral was empty, except for the gray Manx that had given birth to a litter in a cardboard box blown into a corner. The horse tolerated the mewing as long as Charlie slipped her a few oats. When old lady Crawford was alive, the nag had been a racehorse with a personal groomer. Hazel Crawford had co-owned the horse with an unscrupulous District Judge, and for a few years they had traveled the New Mexico circuit. The horse came in first place several times at Santa Fe Downs. Then the jockeys started fixing the races and dragged everyone down.

Hazel Crawford had owned the ranch in its glory days. The surrounding land was sparsely populated, there being more coyotes than people. A crack shot with a rifle, she hated trespassers. Without warning, she was apt to wing one their way to shoo them off. One time the old lady shot a man for running naked through her property. Hazel was less than five feet tall and didn't weigh much more than a hundred pounds, as tough a cowgirl as Annie Oakley. Previously, she ran a brothel in Santa Fe and a popular bar called La Taverna. At the latter, she introduced country music. It was rumored she maintained another brothel in the town of

Golden, a little ways up Highway 14, in two trailers behind the local tavern. On weekends she returned to the ranch to catch up on chores and help the mares deliver foals. She rode her horse with the best of them, pulling off the saddle like it weighed nothing.

If she'd had her way, Hazel Crawford would have left this earth fighting. She never believed in doctors, preferring to cure ailments with country medicine and the Two B's—bed rest and Budweiser, followed by a Jim Beam chaser. But old Bud and Jim couldn't cure this one. Cancer caught her at seventy-nine and by eighty had taken her down. To the end, every morning she woke up and reached for her pack of Pall Malls.

Charlie assumed that the detectives who'd interviewed him were done with him. But there was that scuttlebutt about the lady shrink and he figured she'd eventually come around for some reason or other. He had his alibi down pat about McCabe. Not so much about Bart. Good thing his on-again, off-again girlfriend Brenda hadn't been around for a while. She never could keep a story straight.

Charlie finished his chores. The house was dark. He fumbled with the flashlight, looking for the switch to the generator. There was a loud hum and then the lights came on. He had a crazy premonition about the place. Maybe Hazel had come back to haunt him. Maybe the owner had sent a PI to spy on him. Maybe McCabe had friends who wanted to get even. He couldn't put a finger on it. Last winter when he'd killed a deer on the Indian ruins, he had been dragging it back to the barn. It was dark as hell and he had the distinct feeling of being watched. He couldn't drag that carcass fast enough.

Brenda had felt it too. When he turned the generator off at night, it was pitch black. Fine if there was a full moon, otherwise, so dark you couldn't see your hand in front of your face. He couldn't get Brenda to understand that this wasn't the city, where there was electricity in the house and street lights on every corner. After a while he wised up and bought a case of votive candles. It gave the place a romantic feeling. Chicks liked that.

For the past couple of months, he'd been hearing some really strange noises in the middle of the night, like something being dragged across the yard. One time he even thought he saw light coming from the barn, but he knew the dog would have been barking like crazy if there was anyone around. And the next day, the dog wandered around like he'd been on an all-night toot.

12

Chris Anaya was the Santa Fe County livestock Inspector. A short, pudgy Hispanic man with a military-style crew cut, he spent mornings listening to complaints about broken fences, cows grazing on private land and coyotes killing and eating pet ducks. He patiently took down the information and entered it on the requisite county forms. Afternoons, he visited the homes of the complainants and then the alleged offenders. He was tough but fair. Most people hated to see him arrive. Chris was one year away from retirement and couldn't wait. He had a section of the Pecos River all picked out to spend his days camping and fishing. Today he was headed to the Crawford Ranch to talk to Charlie Cooper about a complaint: his boss's cattle had been grazing on neighboring land. Charlie said two o'clock was fine with him.

Anaya's radio played Spanish music with guitars and accordions accompanying a singer belting out the lyrics. The old Rancheras were songs that epitomized the long-ago life of Mexican cowboys. Not much different than country western music, he mused. Someone's always drunk, jilted or both.

As he soon as he stepped onto the Crawford Ranch, the mangy dog barked. Anaya carried a stash of dog biscuits in his pocket and tossed him one. Charlie greeted him at the door and invited him into the kitchen.

"Charlie, we got another complaint about your cows grazing on the Goodman Ranch. Crawford Lazy C brand on them. On the way over, I saw a section of fence down. Must be where they're getting out. Need to get that fixed, otherwise I've got to issue a citation, and you know what a pain in the ass that can be."

"No, that's not necessary. I'm on it," said Charlie. "I've been fixing up the place, and mending fences is on my list."

"I'll take your word for it. I don't want to have to come all the way out here again," he said. "Hey, can I use the John? I've been taking this medication and can't stop the leaks."

"No problem," Charlie said. "Blue door on the right."

He prayed under his breath that the generally nosy inspector couldn't smell the residue from the load of weed he just cultivated. Charlie liked to imagine himself a cowboy right out of the old West. *If these were old frontier times, I would kill the guy with one shot*, Charlie thought. Anaya probably hadn't noticed anything.

Charlie had picked up a gal named Jennifer at the bar earlier in the day. She sat at the kitchen table leafing through an old *National Geographic*, her sandaled feet propped up on a chair. Around twenty-two, she had delicate features with wide blue eyes, auburn hair pulled away from her face. She was decked out in white shorts and a blue tank top. She stood up as Anaya came out of the bathroom.

"Hey, listen Charlie," she said. "Maybe I can just catch a ride back to town with this guy. How about it, Mister? I have a class at the community college, and I can't miss another one."

"Sorry," Anaya said. "Against the rules to give citizens rides in county vehicles. I can't tell you how sad that makes me." What was wrong with him, anyway? Besides, she was an awfully pretty girl, a little young to hang around the likes of Charlie.

"Aw, who's going to know the difference?" Jennifer asked. "I ain't going to take an ad out in the papers that you gave a stranger a ride in your official vehicle."

Charlie had a feeling he wasn't the first law enforcement officer she'd talked out of something, or into something. He wasn't sure he liked the way things were going. They'd smoked a little weed and did a turn in the sack, but for a gal that cute, Charlie could get it up three or four times. All he could think of to say was, "Hey."

"Well, maybe it wouldn't be too much of a problem," Anaya said. He had a reputation himself for being a ladies' man, but Charlie sure did have a knack for picking the lookers.

"Nah, that's all right," Charlie spoke up. Maybe he wasn't through with her after all. He could tell by that shit-eating grin on Anaya's face that he had plans for Jenny. "I can get you back in time. It's only four."

But Jennifer insisted. "No use you making a special trip when he's going in that direction. Give you a chance to fix that fence, if you don't have to carry me to town. Besides, this guy is going in that direction. Seems such a waste of gas."

"Since it's the end of my day, I guess it'd be okay." Anaya was aware he was on thin ice with his superiors, but it was almost quitting time and besides, who was going to see him way out here in the sticks.

Charlie thought he would choke. "Sure, why not. Make sure she gets home in one piece."

Anaya smiled and shook his hand. "Be sure to take care of that fence, Charlie. I don't want to have to come all the way out here again."

"Thanks anyway," Jennifer said. "It was nice meeting you, Charlie," she smiled and smoothed her tank top over her shorts.

"Shit," Charlie said as they closed the door behind them. "Shit. Shit. Shit."

13

McCabe sat on a leather recliner, his feet propped up on the hassock. At almost six feet, he towered over his wife. His light brown hair was sun streaked to almost blond. His nose had a slight curve from a fracture when he was ten. Without warning, his sister had pushed the wooden swing back to him, knocking him unconscious.

No matter how much money he had in the bank, McCabe remained a blue-jeans kind of guy. He had grown up on a ranch near Kooskia, Idaho, where he spent his childhood riding around the plains helping the foreman gather horses and cattle. He was a cowboy at heart and, by the time he enlisted in the Navy, a seasoned rider. McCabe was pushing fifty-five. Aside from five or so of what he called burrito pounds, he was in good shape and spent time keeping fit.

His father had been the sheriff, judge and coroner of the small town in the middle of the Bitterroot Mountains of Idaho. His mother had been an elementary school teacher. Retired, they spent their summers fishing and camping. They came to Santa Fe for three months out of the year, staying in a small adobe casita McCabe added on to the back of the house. They would be arriving next week.

McCabe had followed in his father's footsteps as County Sheriff in Idaho. He sorely missed his days in law enforcement but knew he would miss his wife more if he took it up again. He was content to accommodate the local Sheriff anytime he asked McCabe to sit in on an investigation. The present case, involving his own shooting, was a little too close to home.

Laura came from the kitchen in response to the ringing doorbell. Rick Romero stood on the veranda.

"Oh, Officer Romero, we've been expecting you. Tim's in the living room." She grasped his hand warmly.

Laura directed Romero into the large high-ceilinged room. McCabe got up to greet him, shook his hand, and pointed to the couch next to him. The room was the size of Romero's entire house. Laura brought in a silver service on a large platter and served them coffee.

"Mr. McCabe," Romero said as he balanced the expensive cup precariously on the small saucer. "It's good to see you've recovered."

"Doing just fine," McCabe said. "Another few days and I'll be like new. Anxious to get back to living. Any news on the fellow who took a potshot at me?"

"That's one of the reasons I'm here. How much do you know about the Crawford Ranch's hired help, Charlie Cooper?" he asked.

"Charlie? Known him since I bought the Indian ruins next to that old ranch," McCabe said. "So that's about a year now. We haven't had too much interaction. I spent the night in the bunkhouse on occasion when I couldn't cross the Galisteo River. Then I hired him to keep an eye on the ruins. That's pretty much it."

"What is there on the Indian ruins that sparks everyone's interest?" Romero asked.

"Well, up to this point I've just been doing some surface exploration. You know, going out there on weekends, digging around. Nothing serious. A few arrowheads here and there, pieces of pottery and the like. I'm waiting for the University archaeological team to come up in a few weeks, and then the serious work will begin. We've done all the grid work and preliminary preparations. I have a pretty good idea of what we're going to find. This is a prehistoric pueblo, one of the few on private property. It's also a rare opportunity to document progress on a dig from beginning to end."

"This might sound like a dumb question, but any chance that there's gold or uranium or something valuable out there?"

"Well, you know, in the late 1800s the hills around the Ortiz Mountains were filled with gold, sparking a horde of prospectors to converge on the area. That dried up a few years later. I'm not saying there's not *any* gold out there, but it's not enough to shoot someone over."

"I wouldn't think you could pan for gold on private property," Romero said.

"If there was any gold, it would be governed by the individual property owner's mineral rights. Sometimes the original owner sold the property and retained the rights. It's all pretty mixed up out there," McCabe said.

"I guess I'm grasping at straws," Romero said. "So far we've hit a block wall on who shot you. At first we thought it might have been a stray bullet, but you mentioned you thought you heard someone nearby."

"Pretty much what I recall. Sounded like a footstep, but hell, it might've been a coyote or a bird." McCabe looked at Laura, who replenished their coffee. "And by the way, Lieutenant, while we're on the subject of criminals. There's something else I wanted to discuss with you."

"That's why I'm here," Romero smiled.

"I'm pretty danged angry that nothing at all has been done about the gallery break-in that took place the same day I was shot. It just infuriates me that no arrests have been made."

"That's out of our jurisdiction, Tim. Anything within the city limits goes to the Santa Fe PD. It's up to their investigators to come up with something."

"Well maybe Sheriff Medrano can light a fire under them. Scared Laura half to death," said McCabe, glancing at his wife.

Laura chimed in. "Yes, if it hadn't been for those nice young men from the gallery next door, I don't know what would have happened. They chased them off into the next block."

"I'm sorry you had to experience that, Mrs. McCabe. I'll be sure to mention it to Sheriff Medrano," Romero said.

Twenty minutes later, Romero stood up, shook McCabe's hand and thanked him for his time. Nothing they had talked about was going to be much help.

"Give my regards to the Sheriff," McCabe said.

"I'll do that," said Romero. "Thank you both for your hospitality. I'll be in touch."

14

Charlie and his long-time girlfriend Brenda Mason had been together off and on for the past two years. Charlie's access to drugs attracted Brenda and in that respect, he took care of her. Charlie liked Brenda because she was a good piece of ass and, next to drugs, that was high on his list. Charlie was content to just be Charlie: drinking, doing drugs, chasing women and smoking grass. That pretty much occupied his time except for an excursion to the Mine Shaft Tavern in Madrid now and then to check out the new talent. The place was always full of hot, willing chicks.

The bedroom was lit only by a small oil lamp in the corner. Brenda sat in front of the dresser mirror towel-drying her hair and working on a roach.

"I'm thinking I want out of here, Charlie." She glanced at him out of the corner of her eyes to see his reaction.

Charlie lay on the bed smoking a cigarette. He took another puff, blew it toward the ceiling, and watched the breeze coax it into a dance.

"Jeezus. Here we go again, Brenda. So, go."

Brenda was surprised.

"Can't keep you here if you don't want to stay." Visible frustration in Charlie's voice caused her to give him a second look. She knew Charlie like the back of her hand. Things flowed peacefully and he didn't particularly care for confrontation.

She had a list of viable but bogus reasons why she was fed up. She imagined he would fall to his knees begging her to stay. She was tired of watching him cultivate his precious marijuana plants. The available money was fun, but he was usually too stoned to go shopping. She missed the bar scene, especially the tavern in Madrid, and hated keeping an eye out for the narcs while he made a sale.

She was tired of working three nights a week at The Burrito Barrel. Charlie could take better care of her than she could take of herself, but the tightwad insisted she work. She was tired of sharing her tips with the busboy, who was not above grabbing himself a handful when the boss was not looking.

Before she met Charlie, Brenda wandered from town to town getting by, hooking up with strangers who let her sleep on their couch for a few weeks before she decided to move on, bored with inattentive cowboys who lacked a faithful boner.

My mother all over again, Brenda thought. She wasn't going to be like her. No Ma'am. Her mother was crazy. Every time her father didn't come home, Mom paced the kitchen, screamed obscenities and yanked Brenda's hair if she uttered a sound. She'd learned to be quiet as a mouse.

Charlie recalled the couple of times he had almost been busted by the damned *beaner* sheriff. It was a good thing Brenda had big knockers and great legs. She was a good distraction to have around. Too bad she had the habit of taking off every few months and then dropping in out of nowhere as though she'd never been gone. *What the hell*, Charlie thought. *Don't have any ties to her anyway. Besides, after my next good hit, I'm out of here.* He was more concerned about something happening to the bricks of marijuana he had holed up in the barn. A few more days and he would be ready to make the sale.

Brenda had a nasty alcohol and drug addiction. If Charlie wasn't careful, she would smoke the weed as fast as he grew it. Sober, she was a lot of fun, even with a few drinks; but when she crossed the one-too-many line, she was a real pain in the ass. One more DUI and she'd be in jail for a while. Charlie didn't want this sort of attention, so he tried to keep her supplied. First she wanted to be with him and then she didn't. Maybe the next time she'd stay gone for good. Jealous as hell, too. Made his life miserable when she ranted about a girl who caught his eye. A couple of chicks he hooked up with a while back in Madrid hadn't come around lately. But what the hell, Brenda was within his grasp.

"Brenda, honey," he said in a voice dripping with sugar. "Bring your sweet ass over here and give me some loving."

Brenda smiled. Charlie really loved her. She just knew it. He wanted her to stay. Pretty soon she could start talking about getting married.

About the time they were really into it, Charlie heard a sound from the lower level of the house. He started to get out of bed. Brenda pulled him back.

"Come on, Charlie, you're not getting away that easy."

"What is going on with that damned dog?" he muttered. Surely, if there was someone down there, the dog would have ripped his leg off by now. He cocked the rifle and walked to the open window.

15

Charlie seemed to be going through girlfriends like water through a sieve. Romero had received an anonymous note in the mail with five names on it, intimating that Charlie knew them all. A couple of girls with no last names, but well known by their Christian names around the bar scene.

On the list was one Barbie Doll, who turned out to be a Barbara Dunigan. Charlie's longtime girl friend, Brenda Mason, herself a bit of a player, had introduced them, much to her chagrin.

Janet, no last name on the list, but Romero thought she might be Janet Leyba.

Bernice, a waitress usually called Bernie. No last name.

Linda Spottsburg, who lived part-time with that crack head Bart Wolfe.

Romero didn't know what relevance the names had to the case. He sent an email to Detective Martinez to go through the missing person files to see if any of the women had been reported missing. Maybe it would help them start putting some of the pieces of the puzzle together.

Charlie had met Barbara at the bar in Madrid last December. She had just celebrated her twenty-second birthday. Loud, brassy, laughed a lot. Petite, shapely, wore her hair in a ponytail, liked fire-red lipstick. Had dropped about forty pounds and thought she was hot stuff, flirted with everyone. Charlie met her through his girlfriend Brenda, who hadn't returned after her last departure.

Barbie-Doll had been browsing through the magazines at the book store in the mall when Charlie ran across her a second time. Their eyes locked. They had coffee. He invited her out to party. Drove to the ranch, the place was dark.

"Hey, where's the party, Charlie?" she had asked.

"You're the party, Babe."
Missing since before Christmas.

* * *

Jan-Gran was twenty-two. Pretty, blond, small, tanned, and muscular. Liked to hike in the Ortiz Mountains. Carried on an affair with her married boss at the old hotel in Cerrillos. One afternoon he didn't show up. She was pissed, about to be caught in a major blizzard, so she hitched a ride to the Mine Shaft Bar. Charlie was all over her, buying her drinks and telling her how pretty she was. Several hours later they ended up at the ranch. Hadn't been seen since February.

* * *

Bernie-Bernice was twenty-eight but looked like a teenager. Waited tables at a resort in Tesuque, a few miles north of Santa Fe. Always introduced herself and added a caveat about the last customer who stiffed her on the tip. To make ends meet, she dipped in the cash register, according to the manager. He was threatening to let her go. She wasn't above hitchhiking home after work, if she hadn't been able to hook up with a customer who'd come in alone. Once, she told everyone she'd thumbed a ride with a guy named Charlie who had a marijuana garden in his basement. She dropped into the bar when she was too sober to face the daily grind. Missing since May 15.

* * *

Charlie met Linda at the bar in Madrid.

A tiny little thing, about twenty-three, wearing tight-fitting jeans. A tattoo of a bird on her right breast showed above her bra line. Linda lived with Wolfe in a trailer park on the outskirts of Santa Fe. Word was she stepped out on him. Dressed in revealing clothes when he wasn't around. Liked to snuggle up as she danced. She was pretty popular with the male patrons of the bar.

Linda liked to look in the mirror. Her hair was thick and long, held with a silver clip at the neck. She told one of the other girls that she liked to apply green eye shadow and then rub it off with a piece of toilet paper. She liked the robin's egg blue a little better. It brought out the color of her eyes.

Charlie spirited her away from Bart one night at the bar in Madrid. They made out and in the early morning he woke up to find her gone. Linda had been missing since June.

* * *

No doubt about Charlie being a party animal. Not interested in small talk. Generally picked women up and, after a few shots of Jim Beam whiskey, hustled them out to the ranch for a few more shots from his private stock. Romero figured that Charlie was living every guy's dream.

16

Lieutenant Romero felt the frustration building. He was going on sixteen hours of meetings, phone calls, interviews and dead-end tips. He swallowed another mouthful of bitter coffee, almost spitting it out on the case file open before him. Sheriff Bobby Medrano had assigned several auxiliary personnel to help him catch up with his case load, and it was an extra task to bring them up to date.

Medrano's office was on the second floor of the Santa Fe County Adult Correctional Facility complex. The windows looked out on the exercise yard, where prisoners could spend two hours each day. The County Jail housed a garden variety of street criminals, locals convicted on DUI charges and other equally petty misdemeanors. The average stay in County Jail was thirty days, but some convicted criminals stayed as long as two years, a much better fate than being incarcerated across the highway at the state penitentiary where the horror of becoming someone's "girlfriend" loomed. Sheriff Medrano ran the jail with an iron hand, having been taken to task one too many times for his officers' misconduct.

He was born in Belen, New Mexico and had been in law enforcement for the past twenty-five years. After graduation from the College of Santa Fe with a degree in accounting, he spent time serving on the Santa Fe County Sheriff's reserve program as a volunteer. For a few years he worked for the State Highway Department as their head accountant, but decided law enforcement was his calling. After a stint with the New Mexico State Police, he became a Santa Fe County Sheriff's deputy and was eventually elected Sheriff in a heated election against the incumbent Sheriff, Jerry Purcell.

Medrano much preferred the old County Jail in Santa Fe. This new location was ten miles from the State Police offices and fifteen from the courthouse downtown. His deputies spent a lot of time going back and forth, delivering prisoners to District Court for arraignments and trials rather than focusing on solving crime. Yes, downtown had been more convenient, but he imagined the County would probably sell the building to some big hotel chain. Santa Fe needed another massive hotel in the downtown area, just like he needed a hole in his head, he thought as he rubbed his temples.

Medrano sprawled behind his desk in the leather swivel chair. Lieutenant Romero sat across from him. Medrano got up and walked toward the window.

"Getting a lot of heat, you know, Rick. You've got a full plate. Maybe we should call in the FBI."

"FBI? Give me a little more time, huh?"

"I've spent the last two weeks fielding calls from the County Commissioners. All these missing women worked in and around Santa Fe. There's people calling all the time." Medrano slid the file across the desk.

Romero nodded. He opened the file and pulled out a few of the papers. "We've got a report from the forensic psychologist. She interviewed friends and family of the women. We've picked up four potential suspects, people they were last seen with. They all have solid alibis. No tips on the hotline have led anywhere."

"In addition, Lieutenant, there have been two shootings in the same area. Are we getting any closer to solving them?" the Sheriff said. "I don't see why you don't want more help on this. Maybe Santa Fe PD can send us some men."

"Damn it, Sheriff, I'm working on it."

"Yeah, but you aren't making any headway."

"The second shooting seems to involve a dispute over a woman. Don't think there's any connection to the McCabe case," said Romero.

"You know McCabe's a good friend of mine. I'd like to see that one solved," he said.

"Workin' on it, Sheriff."

"We've got fifteen missing women in our files. Recent reports point to sightings of four of them in your jurisdiction. Don't you have a spare officer you can assign to check them out?"

"They all hung out at the Mine Shaft or one of those joints along Highway 14," Romero said. He didn't understand why Medrano was on his tail like this. People weren't just sitting around out there, waiting to spill the beans to an investigator.

Medrano gave him a hard look. "I wouldn't say this to the media, but we're stumped. All those missing women and one dead. We've pulled the records of every parolee and sex offender in the state and come up with shit."

"I hear you," said Romero.

"Need some action here, Rick. Bring me something I can take to the bank. Keep looking into those women last seen in your area and who shot McCabe. In a weird stretch of the imagination, there might just be a connection somewhere. Check with the crime techs again. See if anything has shown up there. Have you conferred with that new gal we put on? The profiler?"

"Hadn't even thought about her." Romero knew Medrano well enough to see he wasn't buying that. He had a sly, shit-eating grin on his face. The gossiping elements must be at work. On his way out, Romero stepped into the evidence room and talked to one of the crime scene techs. Nothing new there.

Late afternoon, Romero left the complex. Cloudy skies made it appear later than it was. *Maybe I'm losing my touch*, he thought as he turned onto the highway. He cruised along Highway 14, the Turquoise Trail. There was little traffic as he passed the Garden of the Gods. A group of tourists stopped to pose for pictures next to the monolithic rock formations. He turned onto the county road leading to the Crawford Ranch. His vehicle shook violently as he drove on the ungraded surface. He slowed down to fifteen miles an hour and still felt all his joints rattle. Would have to have the vehicle lubed as soon as he got into town. That pounding was sure to squash the grease out of the joints.

A half hour later he stood at the gate of the Indian ruins and unlocked it with the keys McCabe provided. He sat down in Medicine Rock cave, stretching out his legs. He needed a cigarette or a drink, or both. Something here that we're missing, he mused, but what the hell is it?

According to his last conversation with McCabe, the Indians who occupied this property hundreds of years ago were prehistoric primitive tribes. It was unlikely that McCabe would find anything other than historically important relics. Yet he couldn't come up with a viable reason for someone taking a shot at McCabe. Did they want to scare him off or did they want him dead?

He looked toward the Crawford Ranch. Was the answer over there? Why had Bart Wolfe also been shot in this location? How did Charlie Cooper fit into the equation? Did he have to be on the ruins to check them out or couldn't he just stand at the fence between the two properties? He would have been able to see a vehicle or even someone walking around the ruins. Knowing Charlie, his idea of 'checking something out' would be to stick his head out the door, crane his neck and look toward the sky.

It was getting dark. Romero felt a creepy feeling run up his spine. Freaky. He had the sensation of being watched, as though a crowd of people were sitting in the bleachers waiting for him to make a play. A burst of wind erupted from nowhere, stirring up a dust storm.

17

The phone rang as Romero unlocked the door. He threw the keys on the desk, put the breakfast burrito he picked up at the café in Cerrillos next to it, and reached for the phone. The call had already gone to message. He'd let Clarissa retrieve it when she came in. As he filled the coffee pot, Detective Clyde Martinez and Clarissa drove up. Martinez went into the bathroom.

"Yum. You smell nice today, Lieutenant. Trying out a new cologne?" Clarissa mimicked a fake swoon.

"Shhh, this is serious business here. Did you bring the donuts?" Romero said, smiling.

"What's up, boss?" Martinez asked, still zipping up as he walked into the room, not realizing Clarissa was still there.

Romero motioned Martinez to sit down, offered him a cup of coffee, and pushed the box of donuts his way. Martinez shook his head and patted his stomach, which was flat as a tortilla. He evidently intended to keep it that way.

Romero handed Martinez a package. "Photos of the women reported missing in Santa Fe County the past year. Show these pictures to local businesses along Highway 14. Start at the Allsup's and work your way up to Madrid. Maybe we can get something going on this investigation. See if you can get addresses on any of them, and in a couple of cases, their last names.

"The Sheriff's taking a crapload of heat about nothing turning up on any of these women, and he's passing it down to us. Media's coming down hard. The families are accusing him of not giving a damn."

"Yeah, I heard a lot of palaver about that," Martinez said. He reached for a donut, cut it in half and swirled it in his coffee.

"We're expected to pull a rabbit out of a hat, I guess," Romero said. "If it ain't there, it ain't there. So we need to turn over a few rocks and see who crawls out from under."

"Will do, Boss," said Martinez. "I'll get right on it."

Later that morning, Martinez started at the northern end of Highway 14, where it intersected with Highway 599, and parked his cruiser at Allsup's convenience store and fuel station. The windows of the one-story building were covered with posters advertising beer specials and a seventy million dollar lottery jackpot. He walked through the door past the tall beer and soda coolers against the wall, and the dozen or so bags of various brands of potato chips, candy, mixed nuts and pumpkin seeds. A few customers waited in line to pay for gas.

Martinez asked the clerk at the register for the manager, and she directed him to a gentleman working at the rear of the store. The radio was tuned to a country western station, the announcer hawking an upcoming appearance at one of the nearby casinos by some long-forgotten '50s recording star. Martinez walked back to the manager—a short, fat and suspicious man in his forties with a thick Latino accent, probably Guatemalan. He introduced himself and showed him pictures of the missing women.

"Any of these women look familiar to you?" Martinez asked.

The manager shifted his feet. He continued to stack six-packs of beer into the cooler.

"Take a good look," he repeated. "I'm collecting information on any of these women. Most of them have been missing for around six months."

The manager glanced at his clerk and said nothing. Martinez was beginning to seethe.

"Do you speak English? Look, I'm not La Migra and I don't care if you have a green card or not. That's not what I'm here for. I need information on these women. But if you continue to act suspicious. I will take you in for questioning."

The manager stopped stacking boxes and motioned Martinez into a small office next to the bathroom. Martinez spread the pictures out on a desk overflowing with papers. He flicked on a gooseneck lamp and looked at each photos carefully. After a while he pointed to two of the women.

"This one, maybe I know," he said in broken English. "Come in with that tall guy that works rancho in Cerrillos. Buy gas here all the time. Maybe cerveza and maybe whiskey, I don't 'member for sure."

"What makes you remember her?" Martinez asked.

"Well, she was pretty. Muy Chiquita, and had big chi-chis, you know," he motioned with his hands in front of his chest. "This guy always had pretty girls with him. And this one," he pointed to one of the other photos, "she was wearing shorts and had real long legs." He paused, still looking through the photos. "I don't think I've ever seen any of the others."

"Gracias," said Martinez. "You've been a big help."

The manager beamed and went back to restocking the coolers.

Martinez went out to his cruiser, removed his suit jacket and threw it over the passenger seat. He loosened his tie, sat for a few minutes and wrote down the notes of the interview. Then he headed toward Cerrillos. Maybe he could get some additional information there.

His first stop was at the ancient 1880s Wortley Hotel on Front Street, next to the Simoni Store. Hollywood producers loved Cerrillos as a backdrop for their cowboy movies. The ghost town was definitely a page out of the old West. He wondered if the hotel attracted many customers. It didn't look as though the owners had added many modern conveniences.

Martinez introduced himself to the desk clerk, a Reggae-hippie type with matted dreadlocks, which appeared to be overdue for a good shampooing. A strong odor of pot permeated the room, but unless he needed to involve a little blackmail in case the guy was recalcitrant, he would ignore it.

"Hey." The clerk turned and pulled the chain on an overhead fan so that it ramped up to top speed. "What can I do for you?"

"Detective Martinez of the Santa Fe County Sheriff's Office. I'd like to show you some photos and see if you can identify any of the women."

"Sure, whatever I can do," said the clerk.

Martinez spread the photos out on the front desk. The clerk stared at them for several minutes. Finally, he pointed to one of the women.

"This one. I recognize her. She comes in here about once a month or so, or at least she used to. She and her male companion would spend a few hours in Room 214 and then leave," he said.

"When's the last time you saw her?"

"Around Christmas; sometime around there. I know it was toward the end of December. It was snowing. Her friends had dropped her off, like they usually did, and then they took off. But the guy she normally met here didn't show up that time. She waited awhile and then hitched a ride to Madrid, said she needed a drink. She was pretty pissed, as I recall."

"Do you have any records, maybe the guy's name?"

"Not really. Most of the people who spend only the afternoon here pay in cash. We don't even bother filling out the information card. It's usually all bogus anyway."

Martinez thanked him and decided he'd pass on driving to the bar in Madrid until he was wearing more casual clothes. No use freaking everybody out by driving up in a police car. He didn't expect to gather much information there anyway.

18

A week after his confrontation with Charlie, Bart Wolfe was released from the hospital. Detective Clyde Martinez had been assigned to the case and wanted to talk to him before he left. Bart sat on the edge of the bed, attempting to pull on his boots but still too weak. An orderly came in to help.

"Hope you got a boot jack at home, Bart." The orderly smirked. "Otherwise you're gonna have a heck of a time getting these damned boots off. You might want to switch to sneakers. Maybe a slip-on."

"You mean them sissy shoes?" Bart laughed. "No thanks! I'll find me a pretty girl to help with 'em."

The orderly leaned forward to help button his shirt. Bart pulled away.

"Thanks, but I can do this."

"No problemo," said the orderly. "Well, on to the next victim."

Detective Martinez introduced himself and handed Bart his card.

"I need to ask you a few questions."

Bart eyed Martinez sideways. Deprived of drugs and alcohol for over a week, he was edgy and anxious to get out of this place.

"What do you remember about the events leading up to your getting shot?" said Martinez.

"You mean what happened before I got shot?" Bart was impatient to get this unexpected visit over.

"Yeah," said Martinez.

"Went over to the Crawford Ranch to see Charlie. Looking for my girlfriend Linda. I hadn't seen her since she left the bar with him over a month ago. You know, it seems like she just disappeared out of the blue. Anyway, I figured she had hooked up with Charlie and they were playing house, you know what I mean. And I wanted to find out so I could pack up her crap and get it out of my house," he said, his voice cracking.

"Where was Charlie at that time? Was he at the ranch?"

"When I was driving up to the ranch I thought I saw him walking across the field with his .22 rifle over his shoulder, so I drove onto the ruins instead," Bart said.

"What happened when you got to the ruins?" asked Martinez. Getting information from Bart was like pulling teeth.

"Charlie told me to get the hell out of there. Claimed he ain't seen Linda. Things got a little heated and next thing you know I was in the hospital," said Bart.

"Are you willing to file a complaint against Mr. Cooper at this time?" Martinez asked.

"Don't see any point in it. You guys going to arrest him or just pussy-foot around like you usually do?" Bart asked. He didn't want to get involved. Charlie was going to say Bart came at him with his knife, and they would both get locked up. It was his word against Charlie's. He could handle this thing himself. Get even with Charlie for taking his girl. Son of a bitch had no right to go around stealing a guy's woman. Heck, he was crazy about Linda. Where the hell was she, anyway?

"Well, I'm going to arrest Charlie in the morning," Martinez said. "So you better get your story straight."

19

Early the next morning, accompanied by a young deputy, Detective Martinez drove to the Crawford Ranch. He and his deputy waited at the door for Charlie to answer it. Charlie did not appear too happy to see guests showing up so early in the day. He leaned against the door frame. His boxer shorts looked like they'd never been laundered, although he had on a pair of clean white tube socks.

"You Charlie Cooper?" Martinez asked.

"Yeah, what do you want?" Charlie stifled a yawn and scratched his behind.

"I'm arresting you for assault with a deadly weapon against one Bart Wolfe. You're going to have to come with us."

"Give me a chance to throw some clothes on," said Charlie.

The deputy read Charlie his rights, handcuffed him and led him out to the car. Charlie asked if he could make a phone call, so the deputy handed him his cell. He dialed Brenda's number.

"Hello." Brenda sounded half asleep.

"Listen to me. I've only got a minute," Charlie barked.

"Hey, Charlie. Something wrong—what's going on?" she asked.

"Can't talk now. I need you to get in touch with Joe Snead. His number's in the Yellow Pages. Tell him to meet me at the County Detention Center on Highway 14 as soon as he can get there. I'll explain later."

"Are you all right?" she asked.

"Just do it, Brenda. I gotta go," he snapped.

Detective Martinez held Charlie's head down and the deputy helped guide him into the back seat of the cruiser. Martinez opened the front door and got in. The deputy followed after securing Charlie's door. An iron mesh screen separated the back seat from the front.

Although mad as hell at being arrested, Charlie breathed a sigh of relief that the cops hadn't searched his place. The deputy had grabbed his rifle from the kitchen table, but nothing else. Charlie decided he would be very cooperative.

The Santa Fe County Adult Detention Center building was a long two-story split level brick and cement building. Arriving at the complex, the cruiser stopped at a metal gate at the end of a long driveway next to a chain link fence. The deputy punched in a code and the gate slid open.

Martinez parked and the deputy assisted Charlie out of the car and nudged him to the door. They entered through automatic sliding doors. Martinez handed the arresting documents to the jailer and removed the handcuffs from Charlie's wrists. Charlie was then hustled into the booking room and given over to a clerk named Martha.

Charlie stood silent as he was photographed and fingerprinted. Snead should have been here by now, he thought. Where the hell was he?

His stomach growled as he automatically answered their stupid questions. He hadn't eaten anything since yesterday. Brenda would be hysterical by now, wondering what was going on. He removed his watch and a turquoise ring and handed them to the booking clerk, emptied his pockets, and placed his wallet and some coins on the counter, along with a silver money clip with a few bills, which the clerk counted out and noted on the envelope.

"Is that it?" Martha the clerk popped her gum with a loud crack. If there was anything sexy about her, it escaped Charlie's generally keen eye. She was on the portly side, with a bit more makeup than Charlie cared for. The almost black lipstick lining her lips matched the dark color on her fingertips, and she looked older than the twenty-five years she probably was. While processing Charlie's belongings, she carried on a conversation with the guard standing next to him, fluttering her long feathery eyelashes while she rolled her eyes and ran her fingers through her Farrah Fawcett hairdo. The guard ate it all up. I could walk out the door while those two play footsie, Charlie thought. He kept his eye on the door. No sign of Snead yet.

Finally, Martinez directed him into the interrogation room. He motioned for Charlie to sit, offered him a cigarette and a light. Charlie declined and Martinez fired up one for himself. Charlie slumped in the chair.

"Charlie, just to get the record straight and give you the opportunity to make your statement a part of the record, I need to ask you a couple of questions," said Martinez.

"I'll wait for Snead," Charlie said.

"Just a few vanilla questions," Martinez said.

'Like what?" Charlie rubbed his wrists.

"Tell me what happened when you had the run-in with Bart," Martinez said. "You told Detective Romero you weren't around that afternoon, but we know different, don't we? So tell me what happened."

"Vanilla, huh? You call that vanilla? I'll wait for Snead."

Martinez snuffed his cigarette out in an ashtray. "Why do you want to waste your money on that two-bit shyster?"

"What are you booking me for?" Charlie asked.

"Attempted murder of Bart Wolfe."

"Yeah, that sounds real vanilla." Charlie swatted at a pesky fly that was buzzing his neck.

"Well, just give me a little basic information."

"Try me."

"What were you doing at the ruins on—uh—two weeks ago on Friday around five-thirty in the afternoon? You told Lt. Romero you were at the vet all day, but we know you got home in the middle of the afternoon."

"You know, McCabe pays me to keep an eye on them and chase away the riffraff that show up periodically. That's what I was doing, chasing away the riffraff." Charlie was getting suspicious. "You sure Snead hasn't showed up and you're making him wait in your anteroom?"

"No sign of the esteemed gentleman." Martinez scribbled doodles on the pad in front of him.

Charlie thought he was trying to make up for the crap earlier when he called Snead a two-bit shyster. "Well, I think I'd better wait for him."

"Bart showed up that afternoon, didn't he?" Martinez plunged ahead. "He the kind of riffraff you try to keep away?" He stood up, walked around the chair and flexed his fingers.

"You got that one right," Charlie said. "Mark one up for the super-duper detective. Here's another tidbit for you. Bart was drunk out of his mind. Or high. Or both. He started getting belligerent. Claimed I owed him twenty bucks. And that I was screwing his girlfriend."

"So you shot him?"

"So he pulled a knife out and lunged at me. Then he grabbed for my rifle and wanted to shoot me with it. I got mad and jerked back. It went off when he tripped and fell toward me. I didn't intend to kill him. Heck, I didn't even intend to shoot him. I always carry my .22 with me in case I see a rattler."

Charlie was just getting started.

There was a knock on the door.

"Yeah?" Martinez asked.

The clerk stepped in. "Detective, Mr. Snead is in the waiting room," she said.

"All right, we're done here. You can show him in," said Martinez.

Snead wore a dark pinstriped two-piece suit, a pink silk shirt and a tie. His skin was tanned and his hair combed back into a neat ponytail. "Detective Martinez, we meet again." He gave Martinez an oily smile.

"How's it going, there, counselor?" Martinez gave him a weak smile.

"Great, can't complain," said Snead.

"I'll leave so you can talk to your client," Martinez said, but instead sat down to make some notations in the file.

John Snead was a well known fixture among legal circles in Northern New Mexico. He was in his sixties and had been a criminal attorney for most of his career. It was a lucrative profession, from the looks of the pricey jet black BMW X6 out in the parking lot. His great-grandfather was an old Santa Fe politician who it was rumored bilked native Santa Fe Hispanos out of land on upper Canyon Road, sold it to his Anglo cronies and kept a big chunk for himself. *Cozy little deal*, Martinez thought. Provided a pot of gold for Snead and his two brothers.

"About time you got here," Charlie said.

Snead pulled out a chair, dusted it with his handkerchief, and sat down. He didn't bother to shake Charlie's hand.

"First things first, Charlie. Relax. I'll enter a plea on your behalf and you don't have to say anything. The DA will ask for bail to be denied and that you be held without bond. I'll argue that it was an accidental shooting. If the Judge won't agree to a cash bond, you're here until the preliminary hearing. I've already called the bondsman. You'll be out of here in a couple of hours. Everything's fine, so just relax."

The room went quiet for a moment. Martinez was scribbling on his pad. Charlie crossed his arms. Snead looked at him.

"What?" Charlie asked.

"When the bail bondsman releases you, Charlie, bring me five big ones."

Charlie wasn't sure whether he meant bills or bricks. "What's that for?"

"Retainer," Snead smiled.

"Yeah, yeah. Bring you a bundle of your favorite green stuff on Monday," Charlie smirked.

The guard took Charlie down a long hallway. A buzzer sounded and an electronic lock opened the door to a large warehouse-sized room divided into eight compartments. In each cell there was a concrete slab with a thin mattress and pillow, a steel sink with cold water, a stainless steel toilet and urinal. He could smell the stench coming from the wino in the next cell.

"This sure as hell ain't no four-star establishment," Charlie said to anyone within earshot. He was glad he was only going to be there a few hours.

But it was morning before he was released on bond. He called Brenda to pick him up in front of the complex, and told her to hurry it up.

20

Every year in July tourists converged on Santa Fe like swallows returning to Capistrano. With warmer, longer days, it was easy to forget how long and harsh the winter had been. This had been the second year in a row that residents had awakened in February to a two-foot snowfall with four foot drifts, yet the hard times were easily forgotten once spring arrived and tulips and daffodils pushed their way up for warmth and sunshine. Summertime heat made everyone forget there had even been a winter.

Several events were scheduled in the coming weeks for both tourists and locals. In addition to the ethnographic art shows, there was an International Folk Art Market held on the museum grounds just around the corner from the McCabe residence. This event was attended by hordes of buyers looking for bargains from a country they would most likely never visit. On the final weekend was the Spanish Market, which took up the entire area surrounding the Plaza. It was the only time of year Native American vendors were not allowed to hawk their wares under the portal of the Palace of the Governors, their shiny silver jewelry, pottery and beadwork spread out on colorful rugs and blankets over the cold brick sidewalk.

Detective Romero liked to wander around and look at the traditional handcrafts, retablos, Santos and tinwork offered for sale by regional artists. His sister Maria was a regular participant in the market. Last year she gave him a small carved angel whose dress was decorated with flowers. She said it would bring him a new romantic interest. Romero thought the angel was falling down on the job so far.

In late August came the final event: Indian Market, which attracted a huge crowd. Over a hundred thousand people swarmed over every square inch of the downtown plaza. Most locals stayed home and waited for the Fiestas in early September.

Sauntering up Canyon Road, Romero was amazed how little it had changed over the years. Canyon Road remained a tourist draw, although its eateries and galleries regularly changed names and management. The last time he had been on this street was Christmas Eve. He could still remember walking up Acequia Madre Road, circling around to Canyon Road and seeing the whole area ablaze with lights. Hundreds of walls and rooftops were lined with small paper bags filled with sand called farolitos. The candle inside was lit just as darkness set in and burned for about twelve hours. Local citizens and tourists alike braved the sometimes sub-zero temperatures and foot-high snow to trek through the area for a taste of a Santa Fe Christmas straight out of a travel magazine article. Every couple of hundred feet, the warmth from blazing bonfires gathered small crowds around them. Even then Romero felt the loneliness. He missed his parents and the interaction Spanish families enjoyed. All he had was memories.

For a city of its size, Santa Fe was still a small town. Discovery of Anna Mali's body fueled rumors of the presence of a serial killer in the area. All three Albuquerque television channels kept vans parked outside the County Detention Center waiting for the Sheriff to explain what progress his office was making. He was going to have to come up with something they could chew on pretty quick, but for now, all he said was, "No comment."

Romero came to a newspaper stand and fumbled in his pocket for coins. A headline story reported: "Several weeks back, well-known resident Tim McCabe was shot while excavating at the San Lazaro Indian ruins south of Santa Fe. Police are still investigating whether the shooting was deliberate or if he was hit by a stray bullet."

On page five, a story in the same newspaper said: "Relatives called police to say a young woman was reported missing after she failed to show up at work and left her dog with the groomer. Police say there is no connection with the disappearance of a woman reported the previous week."

That's how the paper reported it. Young girls came and went around here. They quit their jobs, moved in with boyfriends without telling anyone, and eventually returned home.

21

Detectives Romero and Chacon met with the Missing Persons Task Force in the rectangular room at the Sheriff's Offices next to the Santa Fe County Adult Detention Center. Arthur Chacon was in his mid-forties and had worked his way up the ladder to Chief of the Forensic Unit. He was dressed in a neatly pressed white shirt, tie and dark slacks, the standard uniform of the Santa Fe County Sheriff's detective squad. The tips of his thin handlebar moustache were even with his earlobes. He had an avowed penchant for Tootsie Rolls.

Chacon handed out copies of all the information they had amassed, which wasn't much. A few sex offenders were on one list, along with a couple of recently paroled inmates. There were statements from family, friends and coworkers of the missing women. Nothing of substance, nothing suspicious.

Most of the women were young, enjoyed drinking and dancing, seemed family-oriented and were gainfully employed. DNA samples from relatives were taken and sent to the lab in case there was a Jane Doe stored on a cold slab in a morgue somewhere. Photos of the missing women were included in the packet.

Missing persons bulletins with photos attached that had been sent around to Albuquerque, Las Cruces and the Four Corners area had produced no leads ... although Chacon's office had received a tip about Charlie Cooper being seen with several of the missing women at a bar in Madrid in the past six months. He knew Charlie as a druggie who spent his time high on weed, so he was skeptical that the man was capable of any criminal act other than petty theft. Besides, of the losers who hung around the town of Cerrillos, Charlie was the only one with a job. Being a womanizer didn't necessarily make him a suspect.

Romero had walked the perimeter of the pueblo looking for spent shell casings and reported there were none. Until ballistics had been completed on the bullet removed from McCabe's shoulder, they wouldn't know the caliber of the weapon used. He wouldn't be surprised if Charlie wasn't the shooter. He figured Charlie was a crack shot, and if he wanted McCabe dead for any reason, he would be dead. Jemimah Hodge had reviewed the case. He wondered if she had come up with anything. He dialed her number. She picked up on the first ring, before he had a chance to figure out if he was calling her to talk about the case or if he just wanted to hear her voice.

"Yes, hello Rick. I saw your number on Caller ID. What do you need? I'm in the middle of something."

"Jem, I'm at the Indian Ruins and since it's not too far from your place, I thought maybe you could drive over."

"Have you discovered something I should know about?"

"No, I just wanted to compare notes. See if maybe we can shed a little light on the case. I'd like to close it up at some point."

"I don't think that a good idea right now."

"Hey, you didn't think this was personal, did you? It's business."

"I'm working on a case that needs my full attention. I can stop by your office in the morning and we can discuss it then."

"Does that case you're working on happen to have a State Policeman attached to it?"

"Go to hell," she snapped. There was a lull at the other end, and she added, "Look, I've been wanting to go out to the ruins myself. Probably do that sometime tomorrow to take another look at the scene. I'll get back to you if I discover anything new." Jemimah knew she could have easily met him there. She was unsure how she would react to being that close to him.

Of course, he had to have the last word. "Okay, but it's still considered a crime scene, so please document everything you do." He hung up before she had a chance to respond that she wasn't one of his rookie detectives and he didn't have to lead her by the hand.

22

Jemimah hoped some small clue might have been missed in the recent shootings at San Lazaro. Her job as a forensic investigator provided great latitude in her duties, and right now there weren't too many criminals for her to profile. Besides, she needed some hands-on field experience to hone her skills. Medicine Rock was on the edge of the pueblo ruins. An enormous monolith some twenty-eight feet high, it lodged comfortably at the edge of the barbed wire fence encircling the ruins. In the center of the prehistoric site was a cave, a place where a thousand years of wind had eroded the soft shale into a haven from the elements. She sat down on an immense sandstone boulder four times the size of a basketball lodged on the floor of the Medicine Rock cave.

When she reached down to tie her shoelace, the rock shifted with her weight. When she tied the other shoe, the shifting occurred again. She stood and pushed on the rock. It moved a little to the left. Using all the strength she could muster, she rolled the rock on its side to expose a deep hole below, roughly three feet in diameter, a few inches smaller than the boulder. Jemimah unbuckled the flashlight from her belt and beamed it into the hole. A short wooden ladder against the side covered with layers of dust and cobwebs caused her to exclaim, "Lordy, Lordy! What do we have here?"

Unsure of the stability of the ladder, she stepped carefully onto the first rung, clinging to the edge of the opening. Assured it would hold her weight, she descended the remaining steps to the dirt floor. Pointing her flashlight ahead, she could see she was in a tunnel. She hadn't used this flashlight for a long time, but it seemed to have a bright enough light. She walked a few careful steps forward. For about five hundred feet, flashlight in hand, she eased her way through the tunnel, crouching down every so often in case the ceiling might decide to cave in on her head.

As she rounded a small curve, she stopped in her tracks and gasped. Up ahead, a life-sized sandstone effigy leaned against the wall, its eerie obsidian eyes staring toward her. Standing in sandy soil up to its knees, the effigy appeared to emerge from the ground below. The figure loomed ominously, prompting her to consider turning back. She couldn't help but think it was there as a warning. Was there a sentry up ahead? A guardian of the gate? Overactive imagination, she thought to herself. Jemimah flashed the light down to ground level as she walked. At its highest visible point, the tunnel appeared to range from seven feet down to six feet high and as much as three feet wide. She hoped it wouldn't go any lower before she reached the end. She continued walking slowly for several hundred more feet. A musty smell, like damp earth, greeted her. Spookily quiet. The only sound was her breathing. And then, something else ... A sound she recognized from her childhood living in the Utah desert reverberated through the tunnel. Rattler!

Jemimah shone the light about five feet ahead; the snake slowly raised its head, slithered to the left, and shook its rattles. There was little time to think. She shuddered as she reached for her .22 pistol. Concerned that the bullet might ricochet across the walls and hit her or alert someone else to her presence, she hesitated. It didn't look like the snake was going anywhere. She knew that its first instinct was to escape. It would warn her, stay its ground to see what she was going to do, and then either strike or move away. Jemimah believed in desert karma, each creature having a right to live. No human being should kill them, or the act would follow them forever.

She took a deep breath and held tight to the walking stick she'd used to move debris on the floor of the tunnel. It had a V-shaped handle. She turned the stick upside-down, slid it slowly toward the snake—wondering all the while how it survived down here—and held it down by its head until she could walk by. Once beyond the snake, she breathed freely. Mission accomplished.

The flashlight began to lose its intensity and provided only weak illumination. She rifled through her backpack for batteries. Finding none, she turned around and walked back to the entrance. The snake was no longer in sight. As she emerged from the tunnel, she took a quick look around. Nothing had changed. She rolled the boulder back over the entrance and walked to her 4Runner, eager to get in touch with McCabe. Her original purpose for being there had been sidetracked, but she felt ecstatic.

Jemimah sat in her car and surveyed the landscape. She had mixed feelings about this place. It was both peaceful and unsettling. Maybe she had walked into a sacred area. Could it possibly be true that some spirits wandered freely long after their demise?

She drove home in silence as the sun gave its last peek over the Ortiz Mountains.

23

Jemimah watched Laura McCabe's hand brush against her husband's arm. He put his hand over hers and gave it a squeeze. She had grown to like McCabe. He was what she wished her own father had been. A shiver of misery ran through her as she recalled her own lack of paternal love.

Born in Hildale, Utah, most families that Jemimah grew up around were presided over by a husband with at least two wives. Her father was a fifth generation Mormon and had three wives, the most recent being Kathryn, about Jemimah's own age. Kathryn had not had much choice in the matter. Her father arranged the marriage at the monthly council meeting where such unions were discussed and approved. If Jemimah was still unmarried at the age of nineteen, she would be sent on a mission with young men and women her age, required to travel to another country to spread the faith. This could last eighteen months. Jemimah did not relate to her contemporaries, brainwashed into believing it was an honor to be chosen as a bride at an early age. She was single-minded and independent and wanted a career other than housewife or traveling Evangelist. She was aware it would be futile to express her desire to leave the sect, so her options were limited. Nonetheless, she continued to explore various methods to escape her perceived Mormon destiny.

As a teenager she noticed the steamy stares Mormon men directed at young girls her age and it turned her stomach. Young women she grew up with were brainwashed to be one of many wives. There were no boyfriends, no high school crushes, no flirtatious looks, no weeding out of suitors. For the most part, their blossoming youth consisted of puberty followed by a quick, sometimes stealthy marriage. She questioned the lifestyle of the particular sect her father had chosen, but knew in the long run she had no say in parental decisions. Polygamy was not something she understood.

Jemimah had been spared the trauma of groping hands and forced sex. A childhood skin condition resulted in large portions of her face and body being covered with dry scaly patches, not only painful but more importantly in this case, unattractive. Shortly after her eighteenth birthday, following years of treatment by family doctors, she was referred to a dermatologist in Las Vegas, Nevada. It was the first good thing that had ever happened to her.

The five hour trip began early in the morning. Jemimah, her birth mother, and one of the other wives climbed into the Ford station wagon. Her mother told her to take an extra change of clothes in case they had to stay overnight. Jemimah secreted two outfits in her suitcase, along with money from a savings box hidden in the top shelf of the pantry. She was certain this would be her one and only chance of escape. She refused to think about failure and what would happen if she had to return to Hildale and explain the missing money.

In Las Vegas they found the medical compound easily enough. Hannah, the other wife, dropped them off at the doctor's office and went off to find a dry goods store to purchase bolts of cotton material. The doctor examined Jemimah and gave her a sample box of a new medicine that he said would clear up her skin within a few weeks. She and her mother returned to the waiting room to wait until the desk clerk provided them with billing and drug information. Jemimah feigned an upset stomach and claimed she had to go the women's room, which was up another floor. Her mother intended to accompany her, but the clerk asked her to fill out insurance forms. Jemimah sighed in relief and ran up the stairs. Instead of going to the restroom, she exited through a side door, praying she would not set off the alarm system.

Outside, she ran down the steps and out into the busy street. She leaned against the exterior wall of the building, momentarily exhilarated and at the same time terrified she would not be able to pull off her escape plan. She scanned the parking lot to make sure Hannah had not yet returned to pick them up. Then she took off running. Two blocks, maybe three. She jumped on a city bus, not caring where it went. She rode for five or six blocks, asked the driver for directions, and then exited, crossed the street and took another bus to the Greyhound Bus terminal where she bought a ticket to Los Angeles.

Two hundred and fifty long miles later, she was in LA. She found her way to the women's restroom and sliced off her waist length hair with scissors taken from the sewing basket at home. She didn't care how she looked, as long as it changed her appearance enough so that she would not be recognized. Later that day she located a one-room efficiency apartment, and a few days later she was hired as a sandwich person in a popular deli.

At the end of two weeks, staring back at her from her bathroom mirror was a clear, clean complexion. The new prescription had worked. She had gone from a somewhat plain Jane to a beautiful young woman. Jemimah relegated her childhood to a compartment in the back of her mind and carved out her future. She figured the family had promptly ostracized her. Now, after all these years, she finally felt safe, and much too old to be of any interest to lecherous old Mormon men.

"Do you have family?" said McCabe, popping her back into the present.

"No, I don't. Lost them a long time ago." Jemimah pushed the rush of bitterness back.

"Well, come and visit us any time you want, dear." Laura McCabe placed a warm hand on hers.

"I'd like that," said Jemimah. For the first time in her life, she felt welcome.

"Okay, Jemimah, let's get down to brass tacks here," McCabe said. "You said you were out at the ruins, looking around, something about a tunnel. Fill me in."

"Yes, sir," she smiled. "Be glad to. Yesterday I was walking around the ruins, searching the cave area on the off chance we might have missed something that might connect with your shooting. I sat down on that big boulder in the corner to tie my shoelaces."

"Yes, I know the one," McCabe nodded.

"Well, when I sat down, the rock seemed to shift, so I rolled it over and found it had been covering the entrance to a tunnel down below."

"You're kidding me," said McCabe.

"I think you need to see it for yourself. There was a ladder ..."

"What kind of ladder?" McCabe could not conceal his excitement. "What was it made of?"

"The ladder? It was wood, much like those Coyote ladders you see outside the trading posts on the highway. Only much older. I only went in a little ways. I thought I'd better get back and give you a call, it being your property and all. I'd love to go back there with you and look around. Probably has nothing to do with your case but I'm intrigued."

"Heck, it's too late tonight. How about tomorrow, if you like? I know I won't sleep a wink. I'd darn sure like to see what you're describing. How about I meet you there early tomorrow morning, preferably at the crack of dawn?"

"Maybe she's not an early riser," laughed Laura.

"No, no. That's perfect. I get up early to feed Mandy— my appaloosa. I'll be there. And on another note, I was wondering if I might impose on you to help me out. Not just with your case. You may be able to give me some insight into missing person reports filed within the last six months."

"Whatever I can do. By the way, congratulations on your new job. I didn't realize that when you found me it would turn into a career."

"Neither did I. It's turning out to be more than I bargained for. There's so much to learn. Aside from law enforcement, most of my career as a psychologist has been in private practice."

McCabe was genuinely pleased to be asked for advice on a case. "How's about we meet at the ruins, spend a few hours there and then have a late breakfast at the San Marcos Café?"

Laura rolled her eyes and smiled. "What's that old saying about not being able to change the stripes on a tiger?" she said. "He's been wanting to get his feet wet again in law enforcement. Just don't go letting him get in too deep."

"We're just going to snoop around a little bit, Honey," said McCabe. "I doubt there's much danger in that. And you know I can't get into trouble looking through old case files."

"I'll keep a close eye on him," Jemimah winked at Laura. "Tomorrow will be just fine," she told McCabe.

"I look forward to it," he said, not containing his excitement.

Driving home, Jemimah thought about Rick and where their relationship was headed. She did not want it to move too fast. She wasn't sure she liked him better than Whitney, but then again she wasn't sure she liked Whitney at all ... well, other than his very handsome looks, his macho ways, and his concern for her welfare. She had been uneasy about dating again, particularly someone in law enforcement, and now she had two suitors who were cops. She hadn't been on an official date with either, but she had spent time with each. Jeff Whitney was strong minded and forward. She knew exactly what he wanted and it made her blush to think about it. With Rick Romero, she had to read between the lines. He was intense where work was concerned, but warm and sensitive around her. A charismatic tenderness, and it unnerved her.

Over the last five years she had spent many hours on a therapist's couch, delving into the difficulties she experienced after leaving her family and striking out on her own. After a whirlwind courtship in college, she married Dustin Peters, a pre-med student from Delaware. It didn't take long to discover he was a control freak, much like her father. The marriage ended in divorce, inflicting another blow to her already damaged self-esteem. After that, she threw herself into her career, grasping for every brass ring she could reach. There were few goals she hadn't yet accomplished; one of them was the ability to see a relationship through for more than a few months. Rick had also spoken about his failed marriage, so they each had a major relationship strike against them. Maybe that was good; they would be less likely to jump into anything without thinking. Right now she was making it impossible for them to enjoy each other's company. She was mystified as to why he continued to pursue her. On a subconscious level, she had pushed him away every time he moved too close. Oh, who the hell was she kidding? She was pretty sure she had blown all her chances with him.

The sun was setting, bringing with it a mild drop in temperature. A chill ran through her. She was exhausted.

24

Jemimah reached into her pocket for a wad of Kleenex and sneezed again. She was allergic to almost everything in the air and it dampened her excitement about spending more time out on the Indian ruins. The juniper and chamisa were in full bloom and the winds pushed and dragged their pollen into every corner. It was an hour past dawn. She waited for McCabe to drive up. Two ravens flew overhead twittering and squawking at her unwelcome presence.

Ten minutes later, a cloud of dust in the distance came into view, with McCabe's silver Hummer just ahead of it. He drove up to the fence, parked next to her Toyota and waved her over as he unlocked the gate. Tossing his baseball cap into the backseat of the Hummer, he grabbed several battery powered lanterns and a flashlight.

"Okay, Jemimah," he said. "Let's get cracking! I can't wait to see what you discovered."

They walked up the short incline to the high shallow cave at Medicine Rock. She pushed on the boulder to show him how it moved. McCabe whistled and together they rolled the rock over on its side.

"Unbelievable. I've sat on that rock a hundred times. Let's see what else we can find. Holy smokes, I feel like a kid on a scavenger hunt!" he chuckled.

"Lead the way," Jemimah said.

McCabe handed her one of his lamps. She followed closely behind him once they descended the rungs of the ladder.

"It's not so dark here," she said. "But it will be farther on." She kicked herself for making such a dumb statement.

Jemimah was giddy as a ten-year-old as they embarked on their adventure. She hoped they would encounter great treasures stored for centuries in the depths of the cave. She held on to McCabe's belt loop as they trudged ahead, beyond the point where she encountered the rattler. She told McCabe that the effigy that had frightened her was up ahead. She hadn't known how to describe it, and now he stood two feet from it.

"My God," he said. "I can't believe my eyes. This is unlike anything I expected to find on these ruins. I have to show this to Laura." He snapped a quick photo with his digital camera.

They continued on, McCabe positioning the two lanterns so that one shone forward and the other upward. Jemimah directed the beam of her flashlight downward, the memory of the snake momentarily crossing her mind.

"I think this is where my batteries gave out" she said. "It's as far as I went before I turned back." They continued forward, McCabe in a state of total amazement at these new underground surroundings. They walked in silence for a few minutes.

"I figure we're about a thousand feet in," McCabe said. "It's hard to gauge, particularly since we're not moving at a steady pace. The shaft seems to continue on ahead of us. Can't tell how far it goes into the earth."

Jemimah walked into a large cobweb and stifled a scream. She hoped McCabe would not think her a scaredy-cat, but the cobweb had caught her off guard. Oh hells bells, she was a scaredy-cat, no denying it. She was glad she hadn't ventured this far alone.

"Watch your head there, Jemimah. The ceiling drops off a short distance up ahead, and there's a little bit of an incline."

They continued at a slow pace. McCabe leaned down to pick up a small brown piece of bone. "A flute!"

Jemimah could detect the excitement in his voice, although she saw nothing exciting about a musical instrument. She doubted the Indians had flutes, but then, what did she know about their culture?

"What would they use a flute for? They didn't have chamber music, did they?"

"Awesome." McCabe was kind enough not to give her the you-idiot look. "This little flute was probably used to make bird calls," he said. "Maybe to woo an Indian maid. This is no time to stop and gawk. I still can't help wondering why they dug this tunnel. Maybe to hide from marauding enemies? Damn, I can't wait to get back down here with some real lighting equipment."

Jemimah shuddered, she almost walked into another stringy web, where a huge black spider was knitting its way toward the ceiling. McCabe swatted with his leather glove and stepped on it, grinding it under his boot.

"Under ordinary circumstances I wouldn't have done that. I imagine some of these critters have been hanging around in here for a long time, but we can't afford to be bitten right now," he said. "Ahead of us, the ground seems to be pretty virginal. No footprints that I can make out. I doubt if anyone has been down here in a long, long time. Nothing has been disturbed."

They seemed to have walked for a mile. Jemimah felt closed-in. She could feel her heart racing. Was it just from the lack of oxygen? Years ago she visited Carlsbad Caverns in southern New Mexico and walked through the massive caves and tunnels. She remembered the guide assuring them there was plenty of oxygen to go around. Hold that thought, she told herself. She traipsed behind McCabe, using as many mind-calming techniques as she could remember from sessions with her shrink. She was conscious of every breath. At least she wasn't alone this time. She wouldn't have gone this far even if her flashlight hadn't given out.

"Man oh man, I'm speechless," said McCabe. "How you doing there, Jemimah?"

She jumped as McCabe's voice brought her back to the present. "Whew … all right. I imagine you have a lot of unanswered questions."

"That's an understatement if I ever heard one," he chuckled.

A few feet ahead they encountered a small alcove that appeared to be about six foot square.

"Half a dozen people could easily stand in here," he said. "What do you think, Jemimah, shall we keep going? For all we know this tunnel might go all the way to Galisteo."

"That's more than five miles," she said, stifling a need to hyperventilate.

"Unless there are air vents that have been covered up all these years, it's unlikely that it could go that far," McCabe said. A mining shaft can go pretty far into a mountain, but this is nowhere large enough for that."

"It seems to be just high enough to walk upright, though," Jemimah said.

"Yes, and from the research I've done, the Tano were short in stature like many Pueblo Indians. If that were true, it doesn't account for the tunnel not being much over six feet in height." There was only about a foot between the ceiling of the tunnel and McCabe's head.

"Maybe they had to allow for carrying torches?" she offered.

"By gosh, Jemimah, you could be right," he said.

As they rounded a slight turn in the tunnel, a strong odor assailed them both. McCabe put his arm out abruptly, stopping Jemimah in her tracks and almost knocking her over.

"Jemimah," he said, raising his voice. "Go back to the entrance and call Detective Romero."

"What is it? What's there?" she said, shining her light up ahead. "Oh, my God," she swallowed deeply to stifle a scream that insisted on emerging from her throat. Five feet ahead they could see several bodies, all seated on the floor, propped up against the wall of the tunnel. They were in various stages of decomposition—no way to tell by their appearance how long they'd been there. The stench was overwhelming. It was all she could do to keep from vomiting. Jemimah stood silent, petrified, as though her legs had suddenly become rooted like a Yucca plant.

"Jemimah," McCabe said firmly. "Go back to the car and call Romero. Tell him what we've found and to get out here, *pronto!*"

"You're not going to stay here alone, are you?" she stammered.

"Well, they *are* dead," McCabe said dryly. His long career as a Sheriff in Idaho kept him from reacting otherwise. "Jemimah, do as I ask. I'll go up a ways and see if there's anything else. Maybe there's an exit or, God forbid, more bodies. I know this is a crime scene, but I'm just going to go a little way in and then turn back. My tracks will be obvious."

Jemimah spun around, feeling the tunnel begin to close around her. Her entire body was shaking, her muscles weak from shock. It had to be like having the lid slammed on your coffin while you were still alive.

Dumbfounded, she raced back through the tunnel. She couldn't move fast enough. Her knees knocked against each other like castanets shaken by a flamenco dancer. She wanted to barf. She had seen pictures of dead bodies before, victims of the criminals she profiled, but never in a setting like this one, never with so much foul air surrounding them. She was gasping for breath as she saw the outdoor light shining through the entrance up ahead. She scaled the four rungs of the ladder. In her panic, she tripped and lost her footing. She landed spread-eagled in the dirt, skinning the palms of her hands. Momentarily disoriented, she picked herself up. She was still feeling lightheaded as she opened the door of her Toyota and reached for the cell phone in her purse.

She dialed Romero's number. The phone rang six times and then went to message. "Dammit, Rick," she said. Where are you?"

She misdialed the office number, took a deep breath and dialed again. Clarissa answered.

"Sheriff's Department, how can I help you," she said.

"Clarissa, I need to talk to Rick Romero. Do you know where he is?"

"Whoa, Jemimah. Slow down. He's between here and the main office," she said.

"Can you patch me into him?" she said. "It's urgent."

"Sure thing; hold a second," Clarissa said, acutely aware of the urgency in Jemimah's voice. She had never heard her in such a state. Her voice normally had a sweet, soothing, velvety tone.

Jemimah waited on the line. She was trembling and her knees were weak, but at least she hadn't passed out from the shock of seeing the bodies. Thank goodness she hadn't eaten breakfast. She would have hurled it all over McCabe. The phone beeped intermittently for what seemed like ten minutes, though she knew it was less. Rick finally came on the line.

"Detective Romero here," he said.

"Rick, I need you to get to the San Lazaro ruins right away," she said, running her words together.

"What's going on, Jemimah? You sound out of breath. Are you all right?"

"I'm at the ruins with McCabe," she said.

"Is he all right?"

"Yes, yes. Listen to me." Jemimah braced herself on the door of the Toyota. "I can't explain it now. We found a tunnel. He's still down there. There are bodies, and it's pretty awful. Please hurry!"

"On my way. Get into your car and lock the door. Keep the motor running in case you have to get the hell out of there. McCabe can take care of himself. I'll be there as fast as I can." He wasn't sure she was strong enough to be around the scene she described.

Romero hung up the phone and radioed headquarters. He instructed the dispatcher to get in touch with the State Police and the Coroner. He gave directions to the Indian ruins and then dialed Detective Chacon's number.

"Artie, you're not going to believe this," he said. "I just got a call about some bodies discovered out at the Crawford Ranch Indian ruins. Meet me there."

"I'll be right behind you," Chacon said, throwing his car into overdrive and pulling a u-turn in the middle of the highway.

25

A seasoned law enforcement veteran, McCabe tied his handkerchief over his nose and mouth and walked past the bodies. What else lay ahead? Jeezus, could there be more bodies? He shined the light at the cave floor, seeking out crannies and nooks. He was tempted to plunge forward a short distance to see what else might turn up. He would only take a moment, and then he'd head back and check on Jemimah. Women put up a strong front, even when they were trembling like mice pursued by the butcher's wife.

McCabe continued another hundred feet down the tunnel then stopped. He heard muffled voices, words indistinguishable. He turned one lantern off and pointed the other just ahead of his feet, dimming it to cut down the radiance. Walking slowly a step at a time, he viewed what he thought was the end of the tunnel. A hint of daylight seeped through. At the end of a small ramp, he eyed a metal grate. A mound of hay on the ramp was visible. Some had spilled through the grate.

McCabe thought he recognized Charlie Cooper's voice, standing fairly close to the grate, arguing with a woman. He still could not make out what they said. He was careful to not make any noise. The voices became increasingly muffled as they moved away from the opening where McCabe stood.

* * *

"I told you already, Brenda; I'm cutting out of here as soon as I get my shit together."

"Come on, Charlie. Let me go with you. What's it going to hurt? You know how I feel about you."

"Look, it's not going to work out. It's over between us and I don't want to talk about it anymore."

"Charlie, at least let me take you to the airport. You can't leave me without transportation. My car's on its last legs. I'll take good care of it."

Better that the cops don't find his car at the airport right away, Charlie thought. Maybe she could sell the SUV and send him the money. Oh, shit. Why was he being so stingy? He didn't need the few hundred dollars it would bring.

"Oh, hell, all right," Charlie said. "At least that way I won't have to abandon the car at the airport. Once I jump that bond, there will probably be a bounty hunter on my trail." Of course, they'd end up putting the screws to Brenda and she would tell them everything. No point in making it easy for them. But at least he'd have a few days head start.

They returned to the house. He gathered up his backpack and locked the door to the ranch house; then they both climbed into the SUV.

* * *

Back in the tunnel, McCabe waited for a few minutes before trying the grate again. It still wouldn't budge. He heard a car engine start up and then silence. He wound his way back out to the other end of the tunnel. By the time he reached the entrance and climbed the ladder into the sunlight, he, too, was shaken and exhausted. Shielding his eyes from the brightness, he saw Jemimah, huddled in her car.

"Did you reach Romero?" he asked, wiping the sweat from his face.

Jemimah pulled a bottle of water from the ice chest and handed it to McCabe. "They're on their way."

"That was pretty intense. Thanks." He took the bottle and sat down on the running board.

26

Romero sped down Highway 14, sirens and lights turned off. He cursed as he turned onto the dry washboard road, which seemed to slow him down more than usual. His vehicle fishtailed as he pushed forward, but he persisted. As he drove under the railroad trestle, the going was smoother, but the curves slowed him down almost as much as the rough road. Finally, just ahead of him he could see McCabe's Hummer and Jemimah's SUV. He parked a short way up the hill by the fence to make room for the other law enforcement officers who would be arriving soon.

One o'clock in the afternoon. Today was the feast of Saint Anne, patron saint of women. At nearby Santa Ana Pueblo, the event would be celebrated with food, music and dancing. More important, they would beat the drums for the Harvest Dance, which gave life to forces that provided sustenance. Women wore brightly painted tablitas around their heads and men with colorful gourd rattles in their hands chanted to the accompaniment of native drums. Detective Romero was fairly certain the rest of the celebration would be called off as soon as they got news of this latest discovery.

As he closed the door of his vehicle, Jemimah ran up to him. She looked pale and deprived of her usual aplomb. He gave her a quick hug, walked her back to her car, and asked her to wait while he talked to McCabe. After offering McCabe a quick handshake, he got down to business.

"What did you find, Tim?" Romero said.

"Come with me." McCabe led him to the entrance of the tunnel and handed him a light. They descended the ladder.

"Just up ahead here," McCabe said, after they were in the tunnel for some time. "Keep your head down as we go around the bend here. The ceiling drops a bit."

The odor was noticeable after the next turn in the cave and grew steadily stronger before Romero saw the first body. He pulled a handkerchief out and held it to his nose.

"Ahead." McCabe pointed his flashlight at the dark hole before them. "There's two on the floor and two more lined up against the wall."

"Jesus Christ Almighty." Romero coughed into his handkerchief. The odor was so strong he could taste it in the back of his throat. "What the hell went on here?" He knelt and took a closer look at the first body, shining his flashlight around the torso and then the legs. A young woman, maybe in her twenties. He moved the light to her face and hair. Blue lapis and silver earrings dangled from pierced ears. A matching pendant on a silver chain circled what was left of her neck. The murder weapon had cut right above it.

"Let's get out of here. The rest of the team should have arrived by now. I'd like to take a statement from you while it's fresh in your mind, Sheriff." Romero was referring to McCabe's long career in law enforcement.

When they reached the exit to the tunnel, the crime scene unit was approaching the gate. Chacon was already out of his vehicle and coming toward them. There had been no need for his siren to wail on the trip from Santa Fe, but he liked the sound of it and the respect it garnered from motorists and onlookers as they watched him rush by, expertly weaving in and out of traffic. He knew only what Romero had said on the phone. Now, he listened intently as Romero related what lay below. Told the victims were all young women in their prime, Chacon whistled.

"Won't be easy to bring those bodies up," Romero said. "The tunnel is barely wide enough for one person, let alone two techs and a gurney. You got any ideas how to handle this?"

"Need a makeshift stretcher of some sort," Chacon said. "Had some experience with situations like this in Iraq." He turned to his team. "You guys get your latex on."

Never in the history of Santa Fe County had there been such a gruesome discovery. The bodies were dressed only in bras and panties, which hung loosely from the skeletal remains. A yellow silicone wristband imprinted with the word 'LiveStrong' encircled the wrist of one victim. One of the techs said sarcastically, "It sure didn't work for her."

Emotionally drained, Jemimah walked toward the men as they stood around waiting for the bodies to be removed. The silence was unnerving. Cigarette smoke permeated the area. Jemimah walked back to her car and turned on the radio to see if she could find some soothing music. Static. She closed her eyes and leaned back on the headrest.

Frozen in time, infinidad. Each woman's hands and arms were staged in a different position. One neatly folded on her lap, another as if praying, the next with both hands behind her head relaxing against the wall. The arm on the last was raised, fingers tied in a "V" sign of victory. The techs carefully placed each one on the plastic covered stretcher and wheeled them out into the sunlight, where a large canvas tarp covered the ground.

Two bodies had badly decomposed, skeletons showing through the skin. They had been dead for a while. The other two were bloated and swollen, their underwear popping at the seams. They had been there anywhere from six weeks to six months, Romero figured, but that critical information had to come from the ME's office.

The bodies were brought out one by one, a tedious task which took several hours. Each body was laid on a strip of plastic sheeting. It was a grim scene, even for seasoned detectives. They watched as each of the bodies was placed in a dark body bag. The sound of the zipper was amplified in the utter quiet around them.

Chacon's generally cavalier attitude had turned somber. "I'll get on this as soon as we get the ME's reports, Boss. What kind of psycho bastard would do this to a woman?"

27

Standing a short distance from the tunnel, Detective Romero motioned for McCabe to come over.

"Tim, bring me up to speed on what you saw after Jemimah left the tunnel to call me."

"Well, I kept going for maybe another couple of hundred feet until I reached the end of the tunnel. The bodies were closer to that side than to this one, but it's narrower and you probably couldn't get a gurney through that end. Toward the exit, there's a about a forty-five percent incline and a metal grate above. I could hear voices that seemed to be coming from somewhere nearby. When they stopped talking, I moved closer and saw daylight coming through. It looked like I was right under what appeared to be the barn. Above, I could see hay bales and the ceiling. It was light enough to make out what it was," McCabe said as he pointed to the Crawford Ranch across the way. "See, from this point where we're standing, I figure the tunnel ends over there at the corner of the barn."

"Did you recognize any of the voices?"

"Sounded to me like Charlie Cooper. I've talked to him on and off over the past nine months. His voice has a bit of a southern drawl to it."

"The ranch hand," Romero said.

"Yes, and it seemed like he was talking to a woman. The voices were muffled. I couldn't make out much of their conversation, but he kept saying 'no' about something."

"How long were you down there?"

"I waited about ten minutes after they left before I pushed up the grate, but there was something holding it shut and it wouldn't budge. Finally I heard a vehicle drive away and figured I'd better get back to Jemimah."

"Damn, we probably passed whoever it was as we were coming in." Romero grabbed his phone from the cruiser. He dialed the State Police asking for Police Chief John Suazo.

A gruff voice answered. "Suazo, here."

"John, this is Lieutenant Romero, SFCSD. How you doing?"

"Not bad, Rick. What's up?"

"We're putting out a BOLO on one Charlie Cooper, but I need you to check whether the State Police helicopter can take a cruise up Highway 14 toward Albuquerque and see if they can spot his car, a white SUV, New Mexico License plate number KRX-061. Last seen heading south on Highway 14, destination very possibly the Albuquerque airport."

"Is the guy a suspect?" said Suazo.

"He's a person of interest in what appears to be multiple murders just discovered at the Crawford Ranch on Highway 14," said Romero. "One of your people is here, and he can fill you in later."

"Will do," said Suazo. "We've got a 'copter in that area. I'll get right back to you."

Romero stood next to McCabe, looking at the corpses.

"Fairly small women; I doubt if any of them weighed much over 100 pounds."

"You think one person could have done this?" McCabe asked.

"Kind of early to make a judgment like that," Romero said. "That's Jemimah's bailiwick, but she's too unnerved right now to give us an opinion."

"Processing the scene will take time," McCabe said. "Why don't you go over and check on her?"

Romero glanced over at Jemimah's car. She sat huddled up behind the wheel. He strolled over and knocked on her window, startling her. She rolled down the window.

"Listen, Jemimah. This is going to take awhile. It's probably best you go home and try to unwind," he said as he reached over to touch her face.

"Okay," she whispered. It was still difficult for her to speak. He could see that the color hadn't yet returned to her face.

"Hey, it's going to be all right. Come on, get yourself together."

28

Another cloud of dust signaled the arrival of the Sheriff's cruiser. Sheriff Bobby Medrano pulled up in his brand new Ford Cherokee, climbed out, and sauntered over to Romero, cupping a cigarette so he could light it. He had dressed hurriedly, his shirt wrinkled and half-buttoned, and did not appear to be happy. He nodded his head toward McCabe and turned back to Romero.

"Talk about getting put on the map," he said. "This crime is already all over the news. A reporter from CNN is flying in tonight. Any idea who the victims are yet?"

"No IDs on the bodies." Romero pulled out a cigarette. McCabe looked at him and Medrano with disdain and made a comment about littering in a historical area. Romero ignored him and went on, "Techs haven't had a chance to sift the scene. We need to get the bodies out of here before the media converges on the area. I'll have someone throw up a barrier on the main road to keep spectators away. It's private property, but who pays attention to those signs anyway?"

"Hell making the identifications without no more than we have right now," added Chacon. "We did take DNA samples of some family members of women missing in the County. We can compare those if the ME can provide us with DNA from the bodies."

"One step at a time. We'll get that when the time comes," Romero said.

"Yeah, and my wife's going nuts right about now," McCabe said. "If you don't need me, I'm out of here."

"Okay, Tim. Thanks for your help. I'll keep you in the loop."

McCabe waved to Jemimah and yelled, "Let's go home."

As he drove slowly up the hill away from the gate, Jemimah pulled in behind him. She could see gray clouds clustering over the mountains. There was a smell of moisture in the air. It would take more than a gully-washer to sweep away what they had just been through.

29

At seven that evening, Romero slid into the front seat of his cruiser. He needed a drink. Maybe he should drop by Jemimah's first and see if she was doing all right. Hell, he knew she wasn't all right. Even a seasoned veteran never got used to seeing the victims of gruesome murders.

He walked up to the door. Before he had a chance to knock, the dog greeted him, barking, spinning around, and licking his face. Jemimah came to the door wearing a yellow sweat suit and sandals. She wasn't her usual talkative self.

"Hey, doggie," Romero said. "There's a pecking order here." He reached across and hugged Jemimah, holding her for a long time. He pushed a wisp of hair from her forehead.

"How are you doing?" he said.

"I'm okay, I think. I don't know which is worse, the pounding headache or the sick feeling in the pit of my stomach."

"You never get used to these things," he said. "You're still in shock. I'm still stunned, myself. Discovering four bodies—nothing can prepare you for that."

They walked over to the couch, which had a red and black wool Navajo blanket thrown over it. The living room was a mishmash of ethnic collectibles, interspersed with folk art whimsy and paintings of horses. Jem sat down with her knees tucked under her, then reached for the blanket and wrapped it around herself. She closed her eyes for a moment.

"I'm all right, really," she said. "I've seen dead people before, but never like that. I can't imagine what their families are going through. Missing for all that time, and now their hope has run out."

"Mind if I make some coffee?" He started toward the kitchen without waiting for an answer.

"Bottle of Scotch in the cupboard," she hollered after him. "I'll take a double."

"That's a better idea." He retrieved ice from the dispenser, put the drinks on a tray and carried them to the coffee table.

"Take your shoes off," she said. "Stay awhile?"

"Sure?" he said.

"Yeah, why not?" Jemimah said.

Since New Mexico was on Daylight Savings Time, it seemed to take forever to get dark. They sat close on the couch, sipping their drinks. Around nine-thirty, darkness spread around the house. Neither of them got up to turn on the lights. They still huddled together, sipping replenished Scotches.

Jemimah finally spoke. "Gosh, Rick, if I'm going to react this way every time I see a dead body, what good am I going to be at my job?"

"Don't beat yourself up about this, Jem. The odds of something like this happening again are pretty slim," he said.

"I know, but it knocked me for a loop. I started feeling a sense of inadequacy about everything. I'm not sure I'm cut out for this."

"Jeez, Jemimah," he said. "You're a psychologist. You ought to know that everyone reacts differently. Cut yourself a break."

"What does that mean? That just because I'm a trained professional I shouldn't have a reaction?"

"You know that's not what I mean."

"Well, just what do you mean? I hate your condescending attitude when it comes to what I should know or do or even think. That's so much bullshit." She got up and poured the remainder of her drink in the sink.

"Hey, I was just trying to make a point that you're being too hard on yourself," he said. "Give me some slack. I just went through the same thing you did."

Molly started barking. Romero thought it was because he had raised his voice, but she was clawing at the door. "Expecting company at this hour?"

"Oh yeah," Jemimah said. "Run a 24-hour escort service here. Men always showing up looking for a hot date. She flicked the light on in the living room and stood up to answer the door.

Jeff Whitney stood outside, carrying an armful of field flowers.

"On my way back from Albuquerque. Heard it on the radio, called Chief Suazo. Said you had quite a day. Thought you might need some cheering up."

Romero stood. Whitney threw him a look.

"Sorry," Whitney said. "I didn't realize you had company."

Romero figured he had to be blind not to see the cruiser parked out front.

"No, no. It's all right," Jemimah said. "Come in. Can I get you a drink?"

"Sure." Whitney ignored Romero's glaring stare. "No ice, please. Neat."

While she was in the kitchen, she heard the door bang shut. Someone had left. She would bet her bottom dollar it was Rick.

30

Jemimah reached out to grab the rope dangling from the cliff. She struggled to keep her footing, but found herself free-falling down the ledge. Her arms flailed as she catapulted down the rocky slope. She looked around for anything that might stop her fall. She continued to tumble, feeling the pain as the jagged edges of the rocks dug into her body. She attempted to scream but found herself voiceless. The bottom of the canyon was fast approaching. She landed on the ground next to four corpses, each pointing their fingers at her.

She awoke with a start. Jemimah often had nightmares, but this one left her gasping for air. The clock on the nightstand said four thirty. Three hours before her usual wake-up time. Still disoriented, she had a feeling she was not alone in the house. She got up and wandered into the living room. Whitney was asleep on the sofa. Son of a bitch. Was he protecting her or making sure that Romero didn't return?

She felt like shaking him, but decided to let him be. She went back to bed, fluffed her pillows and tried to fall asleep. The dream had been far too realistic. She knew it was related to the gruesome discovery of the bodies of those poor women. She couldn't get the images out of her mind. Maybe she needed to see a shrink; she didn't have the tools to treat herself. Dr. Cade would probably not be surprised to see her.

She curled up on her side and pulled the covers over her head in an attempt to block everything out. It worked. She awoke again at eight-thirty, feeling more rested than she thought possible. The house was quiet. She turned on the hot water in the shower and luxuriated in its warmth for ten minutes. The phone rang as she dried off. It was Rick.

"Why did you leave in such a huff last night?" Jemimah said.

"Three's a crowd. Did that bastard spend the night?" He bit his lip. *Serves me right for jumping on her*, he thought, *but she brings the worst out in me.*

"That's none of your business." She slammed down the phone, only to find it ringing again. "Don't you ever give up?"

"Not when the lady is so pretty."

Whitney.

"Oh, I'm sorry, Whitney. I thought you were still on the couch." She peered around the corner to make sure he wasn't calling from her living room.

"Not anymore," he said. "I took off around seven this morning. You were sleeping so peacefully I didn't want to wake you."

"You're a real gentleman."

"I let the dog out—"

"Did you feed her?"

"Sure did," he said.

"I never can tell when she needs to eat. Always keeps coming back to her bowl, even after she's put a good-sized portion of Kibbles away." Jemimah wondered what it was about Whitney that caused her to babble on like a teenage girl.

"Everything all right with you?" Whitney said.

"Just got out of the shower. Standing here dripping wet," she said.

He had a mental picture of her. "Can we have lunch together?"

"Give me a rain check— Oh god, I'm dripping water all over the bed. I have to go."

"Get back to you later, babe." He hung up.

The phone rang again. She picked it up and said nothing.

"Jem, it's me, Rick. I'm sorry."

"What do you want?" she snapped. "Haven't you said enough?"

"I'm driving to the site of the murders to see what progress the techs have made. I'll probably be checking in with the Medical Examiner's office also, although it might be a little early for that. Can I catch up with you later in the day?"

"I'm going to be busy," she said. "Leave me a message if you wish."

Rick stammered, "Well, all right, but I'd much rather—"

She hung up the phone, dialed Dr. Cade's office number, and scheduled an appointment for two o'clock.

31

That particular afternoon was sunny and warm, the temperature soaring close to ninety. The drought continued and the weatherman offered little hope of rain to provide any relief. Everything was dry on this southern stretch of Highway 14. Smokey the Bear pointed an accusing finger as surrounding billboards warned of the high possibility for forest fires.

The air conditioner in Charlie's SUV wasn't working. He banged on the dashboard, trying to beat it into submission. Even with the windows open, the air was stifling and the conversation lackluster. He didn't want to talk to Brenda anyway. She had a way of hanging on. And hanging on. And hanging on. He didn't know why he had told her she could come along. Now he was stuck with her. He should have just left his car in town and taken the shuttle. What did he need this clunker for, anyway?

His cell phone rang. He was preoccupied thinking about making it to the airport and getting the hell out of Dodge.

"Aren't you going to answer it?" Brenda whined.

"If it's important, they'll call back."

Ever curious, Brenda reached for the phone, punched the talk button and handed it to him. "Talk."

Charlie glared at her, then snorted into the phone, "Yeah, what do you want?"

"Snead here. Got some news for you and it's not good."

"Shoot. Can't make me feel any worse that I already feel. Hold on a sec. A little static out here."

Charlie swung the car into the scenic drive pullout next to a sandstone rock formation along the highway and stepped out. Brenda looked at him quizzically as he walked toward a stone bench. She picked up only a word or two of the conversation, which was what Charlie intended. Nosy bitch.

Snead was in a no-nonsense mood. "Just left the courthouse and was talking to one of the deputies. He said a bunch of bodies were discovered in a cave next to the ranch where you work. Like a couple of hours ago. Didn't have a lot of details, but did remark that they were looking for the ranch hand. That would be you, Charlie."

"Aw, shit, Snead. Has nothing to do with me. I didn't kill anybody. "Who the fuck was it?"

"They haven't identified the women yet. Probably prostitutes, who knows. All I'm saying is that the preliminary indications implicate you," Snead said.

"You know I'm not a killer. So what do we do now?" Charlie said, looking over at Brenda. Her eyes were glued to him.

"I suggest you turn yourself in. If you're innocent, we can prove it, then there's no problem. But right now, you seem to be the prime suspect. Oh, and something else. The guy said there was an investigative report regarding the missing women cases around Santa Fe that indicated you've been seen at the Mine Shaft with a few of them."

"Son of a bitch. I've had a few women out of there, sure," Charlie said. "But so has everyone else. That's a darned good pickup joint. A few drinks, a little sex. That was it. I never asked them any personal questions."

"You mean like, what is your name; where are you from?" Snead snickered.

"That's what I mean. No way anyone can connect me to this, no damned way. This is a mistake," Charlie said, wiping his brow.

"Like I said before, you need to turn yourself in, Charlie. Tell me where to meet, and I'll go with you."

"Steps of the courthouse. Four o'clock," Charlie said abruptly and hung up before Snead could respond.

Charlie got back into the car and slammed the phone into the floorboard. Brenda's eyes widened. "What's going on, Charlie? What women was he talking about? You in some kind of trouble? You been seeing other women? Stepping out on me again?"

"Get off my case, Brenda. It's nothing. Ain't none of your damned business."

Charlie Cooper's intent had been to jump bail. Five Thousand bucks meant little to him. He didn't plan on going to jail for assaulting Bart Wolfe. But Joe Snead's call had thrown a monkey wrench into his plans. He knew Snead would keep after him. Charlie would have to call him two or three times with excuses for delaying his trip to the courthouse and assure him he was on the way, while in the meantime he was flying high in the sky over Texas. He sure as hell didn't have anything to do with missing women. Sheer coincidence that he had slept with one or two of them, maybe three, but who knew where they had gone after they left the ranch. He barely knew their first names, let alone anything else about them.

"You asshole, Charlie," Brenda screamed. She unfastened her seat belt and pounded her fist into his shoulder. "I know you screwed around on me. What did Snead say? Tell me. Who were the women he was talking about? Is one of them screaming rape? You bastard, I could kill you."

Charlie took his hands off the wheel and shoved back at her. He started up the engine and the car lurched forward. "Get your damned seatbelt fastened."

Right now he didn't want to deal with Brenda or her violent temper. His tone changed abruptly.

"Ain't nothing, sweetie pie. Snead just wanted to make sure I would be there for the hearing on that jerk Bart Wolfe. Calm yourself down. We gotta get on to the airport."

Because of the sharp winding curves, this section of Highway 14 generally had less traffic on it. Most preferred to use I-25 to get to Albuquerque in a lot less time. This was the scenic drive, but Charlie's intent was to avoid the cops at all cost and catch his plane without being noticed. He'd purchased his tickets through a travel agent in Santa Fe, got his boarding pass, and all he had to do was show up at the airport. He was flying to Mexico City and then to Brazil. After that, who knew what sandy beach he would catch some rays on? He had fifty grand plus change in his backpack, and it was going to last him a long time.

Sixteen miles beyond Madrid, he heard on the police scanner that authorities were looking for a white SUV with his license number on it. Authorities were headed out to the Crawford Ranch to investigate the discovery of several bodies.

"Shit," said Charlie. "They have my damn plate numbers. What the hell do they want me for? I didn't have anything to do with any missing women. Maybe I'd better turn myself in. Damn."

"What are you going to do, Charlie?" asked Brenda.

"I don't know. Don't ask me that. What the hell can I do? The cops couldn't have known I was jumping bail. I'm going to have to pull off the road pretty soon and make a decision. There's a couple of old cabins out here somewhere," said Charlie. "Maybe I'll just hide out for a while."

He drove out Highway 14 past Golden, another ghost town left over from the 1800s gold rush. It looked completely deserted, except for a shanty-looking tavern with a couple of beat-up trailers parked in back. Out of nowhere, the ear-piercing whirring of a helicopter overhead inundated the entire area. It was flying pretty low. Charlie decided he'd better pull off the highway.

As they drove into Dead Man's Canyon, the tall pine trees formed a dense wall on the sides of the road. Somewhere in the distance, the blades of the State Police helicopter continued to whir noisily. Charlie was visibly nervous, rivulets of sweat streaming down his face. Brenda handed him a pill and a flask of whiskey to calm him down. She'd never seen Charlie this helpless. She didn't like it, either.

Charlie clutched the wheel, palms sweating, knuckles white. Up ahead at the top of the hill, he spotted the forest road leading to the cabin. Bordered by a gravel pathway, the pine plank cabin had a stone chimney, a small porch and a pitched roof. There was a window on each side of the front door and one on the side. An old barbecue grill leaned against the side of the back wall. The place looked deserted. A No-Trespassing sign riddled with bullet holes was nailed to a tree in the yard.

"What the hell did you give me, Brenda? I'm dizzier than shit," said Charlie.

"Relax. It was just a Quaalude. Give it a few minutes, it'll click in," she said. "Always does." Brenda had been doing recreational drugs for years. She knew how long it took.

Charlie made his way up the gravel driveway to the back of the cabin and parked the vehicle. He climbed out of the car, reached into the back seat, retrieved his backpack and slung it over his shoulder. He could barely walk. He needed to sit down.

"Let's go in and check things out," Brenda said. "You can stretch out for a few minutes. There's bound to be a bed or a couch inside."

As they drew near the front door, Charlie took a deep breath. The drug was slowly starting to work. He didn't feel as shaky. Brenda stood a ways behind him as he tried the door. It wasn't locked. He looked at her in surprise and smiled. It was a tall, narrow doorway. Charlie pushed it open without effort. They heard what sounded like an explosion and Charlie fell to the ground.

32

Blood was gushing from Charlie's knees.

Brenda screamed. The sound of the blast almost knocked her over. Charlie was on his back, writhing in pain. She looked around the room thinking some maniac was in the cabin. There was nothing but a wooden chair knocked over on its side. The chair had a sawed-off shotgun taped to the seat and a wide string running in an intricate path from the chair to the door knob.

"It's a trap, Brenda. A son-of-a-bitching trap. You gotta help me. I can't move," Charlie wailed.

Brenda looked out the door to see if there was anyone around who might have heard the blast. She reached into her purse and pulled out a Glock semi-automatic pistol and placed the barrel of the handgun under Charlie's chin. Before his brain could register the agony of the situation, Charlie was dead. He slumped forward and then fell to the floor.

Brenda wiped her prints off the gun, pressed it firmly into his right hand, and reached down for the backpack.

"Night, night, Charlie," she said, and walked out the door.

She reached into the SUV for her purse, pressed in the lighter and lit her cigarette. She blew the smoke out slowly. *This is an interesting turn of events*, she thought.

A couple of miles down the road, Brenda slipped into the public bathroom of the campground they passed on the way to the cabin. She washed up, reapplied her lipstick, secured her hair with a barrette and walked out into the sunlight. She struck up a conversation with a young couple from Arkansas who had been camping in the mountains and were about to drive back to Santa Fe. Brenda told them her car had broken down a few miles up the road and she needed a ride. They offered to take her as far as the bypass where it intersected with Highway 14. She knew she could catch another ride from the Allsup's on the corner.

Brenda was confident that if they ever found him, Charlie's death would be ruled a suicide. She read somewhere that the Sheriff's Department detectives regularly botched criminal investigations. So this one would be a slam dunk. Charlie killed the women and then killed himself. Period.

33

Finished with the tunnel, the crime scene techs moved to the end of the shaft and then to the barn. This wasn't going to be easy. The head of the techs radioed Romero to ask if he had obtained a search warrant for the house. Romero told him to continue with the barn and the tunnel exit and he would get back to him.

The techs sifted through straw, hay and manure, following a trail of evidence which Romero hoped would build a tight case around the perpetrator. Each shred of evidence was tagged and bagged. The killer left an abundance of clues. Romero couldn't believe how careless he had been.

The County Inspector transported the mare to a veterinary shelter until the owner returned. By now, half the ranch area had been searched for clues. They hit pay dirt at the water trough. Buried in a shallow hole was a canvas bag filled with women's shoes, clothing and several pair of bloody latex gloves. Through binoculars, Romero pinpointed an old water well half a mile south behind the barn. It was next to a hundred-foot high, ominous-looking outcropping locally known as the China Wall—a large, foreboding gothic mass of basalt where nocturnal creatures sought refuge in the dark of the night.

Hiking to the area, Romero stopped frequently to catch his breath. *Too much beer and not enough gym time*, he thought. A blast of wind spurred a whirling dust-devil straight toward him. It blew the cap off his head. He pulled his collar up to shield his face from the stinging sand. As he walked toward the abandoned well, he relived the feelings he had while sitting at Medicine Rock. Romero wasn't overly superstitious, but someone seemed to be looking over his shoulder, a *spirit* someone, and it caused his imagination to go wild. Since he'd expressed so much doubt about this case, he began to wonder if he had been directed to this place by a supernatural force looking to avenge the women's deaths on this sacred ground. Clues seemed to be lying in plain sight. Jeez, shake it off. He looked back to see how far removed he was from the ranch house.

The abandoned well was filled with debris, some old, some more recent. Romero poked around with a long stick and stirred the trash around. Metal hit against the stone wall of the well. He beamed his light down, but could see nothing. He hollered for one of the techs. They couldn't hear him. He tried his cell phone, surprised there was service. The tech came running with his toolbox in hand. Together they fished out a knife with a long narrow blade.

"Bingo!" Romero said, wrapping his gloved fingers around the tip of the handle. "Take a look at the edge of the blade."

"Looks like blood to me," said the tech. He noted a few long hairs between the handle and the blade and placed the knife into an evidence bag. Romero felt a burst of energy as they walked toward the ranch. He turned and looked at the China Wall. He hadn't noticed until now that it was blacker than black, with only a single ray of sun shining on it. The hair on his arms bristled.

Romero put in a call to Gary Blake, owner of the ranch. Blake told him it would be a number of weeks before he could make it back from Atlanta, and gave him the go-ahead to do whatever was necessary. Romero told him the horse had been taken to a shelter. Blake said the cattle could fend for themselves, there being plenty of feeding stations around the ranch. The dog belonged to Charlie. Romero said he would impound it until he could find it a new family.

"I just can't get over it," Blake said. "Those poor women were right under my feet every time I went to feed the horse. Charlie didn't strike me as a murderer, but I guess you never know."

"If it's any consolation, we don't think the murders occurred in the house," Romero assured him. "We just need to inspect the space thoroughly to determine if there's anything we need to tie up loose ends."

"Sure. Do whatever you have to do. I'm not crazy about coming out there again anyway. Maybe I'll just put the place up for sale."

Romero assigned two techs to go through the house. They entered into the kitchen. Light from the skylight flooded every corner of the interior. In just a few minutes it became apparent that Charlie lived only in the kitchen, bathroom and bedroom. The house hadn't been cleaned in a long time. All available space in the living room was stacked with magazines and old newspapers. Cobwebs filled the corners, and dust balls hung from the ceiling working their way to the floor. If anything at all were out of kilter in this room, it would be clearly apparent. The furnishings were straight out of the 1950s. It was cold, even on a warm day like today. Two large couches and a low glass-topped table formed a cozy place to relax in front of the massive fireplace. It appeared as though the room hadn't felt the warmth of a roaring fire in a long time. With a good cleaning, the design on the Persian rug covering the floor would return to its vibrant blues, magentas and ochres.

The room was divided by a long oak lowboy with several rows of drawers. As the group walked through the room, a sepia photo of a woman dressed in a white flapper dress stared out from its perch on the fireplace mantle. Romero brushed against the music box on the table next to the lamp. A tiny porcelain ballerina raised her arms as the music began and repeated the same pirouette over and over. A large glass credenza housed a variety of ancient relics: stone axes, arrowheads and fetishes, along with bone flutes, medicine bundles and gaming pieces. Romero wondered if everything in this room hadn't been left intact from Old Lady Crawford's day. The glass was hazy with residue.

McCabe would certainly be interested in seeing the material in the case, which surely had come from the Indian ruins.

"I don't think there's going to be much evidence to gather in this room," said Romero. "Doesn't appear that anyone spent time in here. Let's take a look at the bedroom. From what we know about Charlie, that's probably where all the activity took place in the house."

The techs culled a few long hairs from the bedroom area and added them to the rest of the evidence. Charlie's clothes were still in the closet, along with two hunting rifles and a pair of cowboy boots.

"I guess Charlie must travel light," Romero said to no one at all in the empty room.

34

Two days later, in the autopsy suite of M.E. Harry Donlan's office, the four bodies discovered at the site were laid out on individual tables. A fifth victim, found in her home near downtown Santa Fe, lay nearby. Since she had been murdered at a different crime scene, Donlan was going to compare her wounds to see if there was a connection to the other bodies. Lieutenant Romero stood next to the first table, joined by crime scene head Detective Chacon.

Although his title of Medical Examiner had recently been changed to Chief Autopsy Technician, for obvious reasons Donlan preferred to be called an M.E., rather than a C.A.T. A fifty-something Anglo, his acne-scarred face was framed with a salt-and-pepper Beatles-inspired haircut. He was a large man who carried himself with surprising ease. Donlan had a morose sense of humor that usually irritated Romero. His comments and behavior bordered on disrespect. The last time Romero had attended an autopsy, Donlan handled the child's body like it was a rag doll. Romero couldn't forget that.

The year-old Santa Fe County forensic facility was a high-tech morgue, designed for ease of movement. Every precaution was taken to eliminate the possibility of evidence contamination during preparation of the body. Cases brought to the morgue were received in this central area, processed and assigned ID tags. Harry Donlan took it all in stride but preferred the old methods. Slit them open, empty them out, and examine them part by part.

The assistant technician looked to be about seventeen years old. Donlan never introduced him and treated him the same way he treated everyone, as if he were a dunce. If he spoke to the tech, he called him "Hey, you."

"Pretty nice digs, Doc," Detective Chacon said.

"Modern and up-to-date," Donlan bragged. "Makes my life a lot easier. Like the big paycheck, too."

"So what do you think we have here?" Romero asked, preparing to hear a long lecture.

"Preliminary take on these ladies," Donlan said. "Throats slit from behind in a left to right direction. I doubt if they knew what was coming—or maybe they weren't even conscious." He leaned forward to take a closer look. "Pressure applied by the knife is even, as though the killer held them upright with his or her arm. No sign of a struggle. Quick and clean cut, one swift move."

"Cold winter weather kept the first two bodies from rapid decomposition," he continued. "Other two—one died in early spring and the other maybe a few weeks later. Could be as much as six weeks later. The one over there that we're calling the fifth victim—stabbed in the back first. Evidently she turned to face her perpetrator and then got it in the throat with one quick movement. We're running tests to determine if the same knife used on the first four victims was used on her, but it's doubtful. Five wasn't found in the tunnel with the others and even though the manner of death was similar, I don't think they're connected. Once we've examined the wounds, we can tell if an identical weapon was used on the other four."

"You may be right," Romero said. "That fifth one has nothing to do with the others. Nothing to connect them. Stabbed, yes, but that's not enough to tie her in to the others. That's my guess."

"You don't get paid to guess, Romero. That's my job. And it's a more scientific process than just guessing."

"Just thought that there's a big difference between a stab and a slit," Romero said.

Donlan shot him an exasperated look above the bifocals balanced on the tip of his nose. "You see that sign over there, Romero? The one that says 'Quiet.' Right now that means you."

Romero fumbled for his cigarettes in his chest pocket. "That 'No Smoking' sign means you, too," Donlan said. "You guys want to smoke, do it outside. Smoke can fuck up some of the tests. Now, let me do my work."

Donlan continued his painstaking examination of the bodies. The autopsy technician took down every word he uttered and filled a form for each victim as he went along. Each body was assigned a case number and file. Hey You took photographs and gathered biological samples. He was efficient and fastidious, making sure each drop of body fluid was wiped away.

"Did you know that scientists have developed a new DNA test that can identify a killer's ethnicity through some sort of genetic typing?" Donlan asked nobody in particular.

"That would certainly narrow the field in an investigation," Chacon said.

"Yep," Donlan said. "The test will even be able to identify eye color. There's been some real advancements. Can even pick up DNA on a cigarette butt. Amazing stuff."

The detectives continued to stand while Donlan forged on. Romero's discomfort was obvious. Donlan turned to the tech. "Hey You, finish cleaning up this place." Then he looked over to Romero and Chacon. "All right. Class dismissed. You two aren't going to learn anything more around here. Don't you have shoplifters to chase or bank robbers to arrest?"

Romero gave him a forced smile. "Yeah, come to think of it, we do. As always, Harry, it's been a real pleasure."

Romero and Chacon excused themselves and left the room through a side door. Chacon lit the cigarette he'd been holding in his hand. Like a kid, he was relieved Donlan hadn't taken him to task about smoking. He passed the light to Romero.

"Damn," said Chacon. "That's really tough shit to sit through."

"Yes," said Romero. "It doesn't get any easier, either. Just wait until it's somebody you know."

35

Joseph Stibbe was a man in his middle forties, and his trim physique reflected the miles he hiked in the Sandia Mountain Range. He kept his brown hair cut short, and his piercing green eyes were generally obscured behind a pair of darkly tinted Ray-Ban sunglasses. On this early August day, as was his practice once a month, he drove the side roads near the Sandias. Employees of the New Mexico Game and Fish Department were required to make sure that roads remained passable and that gates to restricted areas were secured. Neither task was easy; poachers repeatedly cut through fences with lock cutters to gain access.

It had been a month since Stibbe patrolled this area, which included only a few privately owned cabins. The rest of the land was owned by the government and accessible to hunters, fishermen and hikers. In the late afternoon, he reached the road in front of Max Leyba's cabin. Recent rains had spurred the growth of grass and wildflowers, and both spilled onto the road with a profusion of color. Traffic was light in the area—only one set of tracks besides his own—and those, which led to the cabin, appeared to be weeks old. A white SUV was parked behind the building. He pulled his truck into the driveway, got out, stretched his legs and sauntered toward the door. It stood ajar. Stibbe hollered out for Max. No answer. He shuffled across the porch to the back and checked the SUV. The keys were in the ignition, the windows rolled down. He figured a hiker had parked there while he hiked up one of the nearby trails. Idiot forgot to close the windows. The seats were damp from recent rains.

Max Leyba had recently reported several break-ins at his cabin to local law enforcement. At the time of their last conversation, he had complained that whoever was breaking into the cabin was walking off with his belongings and treating the place like a dumpster. Even the metal coffee pot he had used for years was gone, and the floor was covered with discarded beer cans and cigarette butts. Max didn't spend much time in the cabin, but he resented it being mistreated. He owned a few cattle that grazed nearby, so anytime a thunderstorm caught him off guard, he took shelter in the cabin. Sometimes, while hunting deer, he spent the night.

As Stibbe crossed the porch, a sweet, cloying odor overwhelmed him. He was familiar with the smell. He again called out for Max, then kicked the door open, keeping his right hand on his weapon. A man wearing Levis, boots and a long-sleeved checked shirt lay on his side, curled into a fetal position. Both his knees were bloody, and under his chin was a gaping wound. The pool of blood around his head had dried.

Stibbe gasped, turned, and almost fell in his rush to the door. He held onto the porch railing and vomited over the side. It took ten minutes before he regained his composure enough to dial 911 on his cell phone. He reported his findings and gave the operator directions. For a while he waited in front of the cabin, but then took a seat in his vehicle. It was a few hours before dark. He felt nervous about being alone with a human body and hoped the police would show up before too long. He fiddled with the radio, trying to find a station to get his mind off what he had just seen. No luck. Mostly static.

He sat in his car for what seemed like a long time before a State Police cruiser entered the driveway. Captain Jeff Whitney, a twenty year veteran of the New Mexico State Police force and a friend of Stibbe's, stepped from the vehicle.

"Joseph Stibbe," Whitney said. "Haven't seen you in a long time. Still with Game and Fish, huh? What's that make, about twenty years?"

"Just about, Jeff," Stibbe said. "I thought you'd be Chief by now. Or don't they let a Gringo run the show in Santa Fe?"

Whitney laughed, took a pack of cigarettes out of his shirt pocket and offered one to Stibbe. He blew a puff of smoke upwards and said, "Let's take a look-see at what we've got here. The ME shouldn't be too far behind."

Stibbe pointed him in the direction of the door. He didn't want to look again. Whitney walked through the door, careful to not disturb the scene. When he came out, he looked around the yard and peered into the SUV in the back. The car had New Mexico plates. He jotted down the numbers and called them in. There was a .243 rifle in a leather case stuffed in the space between the back seat and the rear window. While they waited, Whitney filled out his initial report. Stibbe told him what he knew about the cabin and the owner.

The State Police Crime Scene tech crew—a group of respected field officers—showed up first. Whitney directed them up the driveway to the front door of the cabin. They unloaded their equipment and taped off the area from the driveway to the cabin and around the back. Two of the crime scene techs conducted a perimeter search and then focused on the vehicle. The other went inside to photograph the room and the body and found Charlie Cooper's wallet in the back pocket of his pants. For the next four hours the crew videotaped, bagged and tagged evidence, and searched every corner of the room.

The lead tech motioned to Whitney. "Hey, Whit, come here and take a look."

Whitney doused his cigarette carefully and sauntered over to the center of the room. "Before I bag it up, what do you make of this? Looks like some kind of trap. See, the shotgun is tied to the chair with a long cord, which stretches all the way to the door."

"I've seen something like this before," said Whitney. "Never saw it in operation though. Looks like the trap was rigged up so that when the door was opened, the shotgun would go off as a warning. This one might have malfunctioned. The guy probably pushed the door open too fast. Instead of the pellets hitting the door, they blew out his knees. Ouch!"

"I took plenty of photographs," the tech said.

"I'll make sure to include this in my notes," said Whitney.

The shotgun trap was dismantled, tagged and boxed, and taken to the van along with Charlie's pistol.

In the midst of the evidence gathering, the ME from Sandoval County and his assistants arrived in a blue minivan. Captain Whitney led them to the body.

"Looks like this guy was shot through the knees," the ME said.

"You don't say," Whitney responded, his tone sarcastic. "Never would have guessed. What else can you tell us?"

"More interesting, looks like he committed suicide sometime after. Maybe he couldn't take the pain of getting his knees shot out. Hard to say."

"The pain got to him?" Whitney asked. "Doesn't he have a cell phone on him so he could call for help?"

"Don't see any. If he had one, the perpetrator—if indeed there was one—took it away from him."

Whitney whistled. "Real son of a bitch. How long do you think he's been decomposing?"

"Over a week, maybe. Since today is Friday, it will be a few days before we can start on the autopsy. I'll fax a copy of the report to the Chief when it's done."

His assistants marked the location of the corpse with chalk. The ME motioned to them to remove the body. They carefully pulled the body bag over Charlie's head, zipped it up, and placed him on a gurney.

Whitney called in for a tow truck to cart Charlie's SUV back to Santa Fe and began to secure the crime scene. Sometime later, the tow truck came up the hill. Whitney hailed the driver and gestured for him to back up.

Stibbe still looked green around the edges. Whitney walked him to his truck and told him to take some deep breaths. The vehicle report had just come back and matched the driver's license. Charlie Cooper was the person of interest the Santa Fe County Sheriff's Department had been looking for last week. There was a BOLO on him. Whitney called it back in to Captain Suazo, who relayed the information back to Detective Romero.

A spectacular sunset was on the horizon. The red-orange glow of the half-circle sun blended into the blue-gray skies of evening. Lately, the beauty of these moments had been eclipsed by dark shadows.

36

The following morning, Joseph Stibbe took a personal day. He left his uniform hanging in the closet and put on a white cotton T-shirt, a pair of dark Indigo jeans and an old pair of caramel-colored Tony Lama boots. His Albuquerque Isotopes baseball cap concealed his eyes. The shock of finding the body at Max Silva's cabin had thrown him off-balance. The sight was engraved on his memory. He had personally contacted Max Silva early that morning. The State Police would be on his doorstep soon enough. Because Max had a weak heart, Stibbe didn't reveal too much over the phone. Better to tell him face to face.

It took an hour to make the thirty mile drive from his house in Golden to Max's home in Placitas, but Stibbe found the experience calming. As he drove through the Town of Golden, he passed in front of the Catholic Church, a building so white it stood out from its surroundings. He turned onto Sandia Crest Road and followed the winding mountainous road for about fifteen miles before stopping at the base of Capulin Peak to relieve himself. He didn't encounter another vehicle the entire trip. He relished the solitude of the mountain range cradled by the bluest sky he had seen in a long time.

About an hour later he reached the town of Placitas, once a predominantly Hispanic community in Sandoval County about fifteen miles north of Albuquerque. He turned onto a gravel road, which led him to the end of the driveway in front of a pueblo-style flat-roofed house. Max Leyba sat on the porch drinking coffee. He greeted Stibbe with a warm handshake.

"Come in, come in," he smiled and led him into the house.

They sat in the modestly furnished living room. From where Stibbe sat, he could see panoramic mountain views from every window. Max handed him a cup of coffee.

"Three sugars, two creams—just how you like it," he said.

Stibbe forced a weak smile. "Max, I didn't mean to sound so mysterious when I called this morning." He took a deep breath. "There's been a shooting at your cabin; a fellow was found dead there yesterday afternoon."

Stibbe related the rest of his grisly discovery.

Max blew out a long whistle. "A couple of months ago the place was broken into, on three or four separate occasions. Every time I went to check on my cows, there'd be something broken or missing. I was so pissed off about the break-ins that, a month ago, I went to the cabin and set a trap with an old sawed-off shotgun and a chair. The trip wire led from the chair in the middle of the room to the door jamb and then back to the trigger and then to the doorknob. When the door was pushed open, the shotgun was supposed to go off. It was loaded with number seven birdshot. But," he continued, "I thought I rigged it so it would go off right away and the pellets would hit the inside of the door and scare the intruder away."

"Yeah," said Stibbe. "The guy's knees were pretty messed up." He told him the State Police or the Sheriff's office would be contacting him at some point in their investigation.

"Do you think I'm going to need a lawyer?" Leyba said.

"Probably wouldn't hurt," Stibbe said.

After an hour, Stibbe got up to leave. He told his old friend he would keep in touch. Leyba thanked him for coming and shook his hand.

After Stibbe walked out the door, Leyba sat down and covered his face with his hands. "Dios Mio," he sobbed. "I've gone and killed someone."

37

Jemimah walked into Romero's office, a stack of books in her arms. Clarissa greeted her with a knowing smile and pointed to the large cubicle in the corner, where Romero was retrieving a fax. He motioned her over. Jemimah paused to pour herself a cup of thick black coffee, then had second thoughts and dumped it into the sink.

"Hey, Rick. Thanks for making time for me. Thought I'd stop by and see if anything new has popped up on the case." As much as she hated to admit it, she admired his skills as an investigator. She couldn't pinpoint what it was about him that annoyed her so much.

"Still at square one," he said. "Lots of tips, but nothing seems to pan out. Maybe we're looking too hard."

"I have a few theories, if you have a minute," she said.

"Shoot." He swallowed the last of his coffee and tossed the Styrofoam cup into the trash. He wanted to say how great she looked, but she'd probably take offense and go storming out. Still, she was beautiful.

"One of the last cases I worked in Texas involved a string of killings with a similar MO. It got me to thinking about that case. We might have a parallel situation here. Our perp seems to have a rage against women, based on the manner in which they were killed. Swiftly. Somewhere along the way, a woman took away his power, or possibly lost hers. So the killer was essentially recouping that power, leaving the victim helpless," Jemimah said. "Do you follow?"

"Why did you say *her*?" Romero asked.

"For one reason: the victims died quickly without being tortured. A male killer generally takes pleasure in watching his victim suffer. He tortures them with the idea that if they give in to him, they might live. It's just a theory. Most times, we assume serial killers are men." Jemimah felt like a graduate student trying to impress her professor. She looked up. At least he was acting interested in what she had to say.

"I was leaning toward the ranch-hand being our killer," Romero said. He pulled open a desk drawer and took out a pair of nail clippers. He put them back when she shot him an 'are you interested or not' look.

"Charlie Cooper? I don't think so," Jemimah said. "Charlie was a druggie, spent a lot of time stoned. Most druggies are incapable of serial killings. Requires too much forethought. Too much planning. They don't have the ability to focus on that—they're just interested in the momentary high, chasing the next one, or in whether they are going to run out of drugs too soon."

He moved his chair closer to hers. She looked at him quizzically. "Go on, I'm listening."

"From what I learned at the bar in Madrid, Charlie's quite the womanizer, but he has a steady girlfriend—Brenda Mason. On and off for some time now. McCabe has seen her a few times, so I thought of asking him ..."

Clarissa interrupted, animatedly waving a sheet of paper. "Sorry to interrupt, Boss, but we've got a caller on the tip line. This barmaid says she might have information."

Romero wheeled his chair behind his desk and reached for his the phone. "Hello. Detective Romero here."

"Yes, hello. My name is Julie, and I work at the Mineshaft Tavern." She sounded breathless.

"You've got some information for me?" Romero asked.

"Uh-huh, I read that Charlie Cooper's body was found and that the police think he may be the one who murdered those women. Listen, Charlie was a nice man. He wouldn't have done anything like that. He was gentle as a lamb."

Her phone was breaking up. Romero put one hand over his ear to hear her better.

"So, what is it you want to tell me, Julie?" He looked over at Jemimah and raised his eyebrows.

"Some months ago, maybe in April, I was working late. Charlie's girlfriend Brenda got into a nasty fight with one of the victims, I think her name was Linda—the one that lived with Bart Wolfe. Anyway, I was in one of the stalls in the bathroom and heard Brenda screaming at her. Told her that she'd better stay the hell away from Charlie or there would be hell to pay."

Jemimah could see the expression on Romero's face change. He was attentive and professional to the caller, waiting patiently for information, jotting it down on a yellow pad.

"Go on, Julie," he said.

"So a few nights later, I see Charlie with Linda. They're in the parking lot making out. A few hours go by, and Brenda comes in looking for Charlie. Someone tells her he left with Linda. Brenda gets all hysterical and starts screaming that she's going to kill that bitch. And now she's dead. That's pretty much all I wanted to say," she said.

"Thank you, Julie. You've been very helpful. Now let me ask you—has Brenda been in the bar lately?" Romero said.

"Yes, she was in yesterday. Wearing some really nice clothes and going on and on about buying a new car. She claimed she'd come into a lot of money. Didn't even act sad about what happened to Charlie."

Romero was beginning to think Jemimah might be right on.

"Julie, I'm going to send Dr. Hodge over to talk to you," Romero said. "She's profiling the killer for us. If Brenda happens to be there, I'd like you to point her out."

"Sure will," Julie said.

"Thank you, sweetheart. You've been a great help. Let me hand you back to Clarissa. Let her know your work schedule for the next week." He waved Clarissa over.

Romero sat down and explained to Jemimah what the caller had said. "We need to look into this a little closer, in light of your theories about the possibility of a woman being our killer. You may have hit the nail right on the head."

"I'm going over to see McCabe around noon," Jemimah said. "I might bring him along. He's been hankering to get involved, and this might be a good time to take advantage of his experience in law enforcement."

Romero walked Jemimah to the door, careful to not brush against her, lest she conclude he was still interested.

38

All week long, Jemimah worked on the killer's psychological profile. She believed the killer of the young women was a product of an overbearing parent, narcissistic on one hand and needy on the other. The mother probably alternated between expressing love and hate: one moment hating her husband and loving her child; the next moment, just the opposite. The case file was full of interviews with Charlie's friends and acquaintances. Not one confirmed that Charlie had violent tendencies. On the contrary, they made him out to be kind and gentle, even when stoned.

Charlie's brother from Wyoming claimed the body. He told Jemimah that Charlie was the second of three children. He loved animals, football and fishing. He was popular in high school. He dated regularly, generally stayed in relationships for six months to a year. He didn't like to be tied down—liked to travel, hunt and fish. Their mother was a loving woman who attended all their school functions. She died when the boys were in high school. His father remarried some years later. Charlie called home at least once a year. Charlie didn't fit any of the criteria of a serial murderer. Jemimah crossed him off her list.

39

The newspaper business boomed in Santa Fe, with headlines that implied the murders had been solved. Charlie Cooper was dead. Single women breathed a collective sigh of relief. There was no deranged madman walking the streets of Santa Fe.

Voluminous files on the murder investigation sat in a neat stack on Romero's desk. Although he felt compelled to transfer them to the Sheriff's office, he had a gnawing feeling in the pit of his stomach. Jemimah held fast to her belief that Charlie couldn't be the killer. They were getting ready to meet with Sheriff Medrano to summarize the case.

Then a phone call from the Assistant ME moved the investigation back to square one. The tox screen had come back on Charlie Cooper. His blood had a high concentration of Methaqualone, better known as Quaalude, and alcohol. He would have probably been unconscious right after his knees were shot out and the bullet entered under his chin. That much Quaalude could have killed him in a few hours without anyone shooting him. It would have gone down as another accidental drug overdose.

Romero called Jemimah to give her the news. She was tempted to say, 'I told you so,' but held back, instead giving him a half-smile, which of course he could not see.

At ten o'clock that morning, Jemimah arrived at the law enforcement complex, flashed her badge to the guard at the gate and parked next to Lieutenant Romero's vehicle. She walked over to him. Through his dark glasses, she couldn't tell whether or not he was glad to see her. The fireworks between them, fueled by something neither could define, had cooled. Mainly, she felt, because they had not been thrown together much lately. She still had feelings for him but was not sure she wanted to pursue them. She felt overdressed in a dark linen suit, tailored white blouse, and black pumps, but figured that if she looked good, it enhanced her performance. The Sheriff could be a tough nut to crack and doubly tough to impress.

Romero smiled and earned an automatic response from her. They both looked neat and professional. The receptionist directed them to the Sheriff's office. The furniture had been rearranged since the last time they had been there. Functional, but not deserving of any awards from *Architectural Digest*.

"Good to see you both," said Sheriff Medrano. "Have a seat. Carmen, bring some coffee in, would you?" He looked disheveled, as though he hadn't slept in a week.

"Lieutenant Romero, Rick, bring me up to speed on the four bodies at the morgue. What do we have so far?"

"Not a hell of a lot on the victims personally," Romero said, "other than whatever we gathered from friends and relatives. Janet Leyba, twenty-two years old, a secretary at the Hampton Lumber yard on Alameda Street. Bernice Williams, twenty-eight, a waitress at Tesuque Lodge. Her sister said she frequently hitchhiked around town. Barbara Dunigan, twenty-two. Worked at a high-end jewelry shop in downtown Santa Fe. Last, Linda Spottsburg, twenty-three. Worked at odd jobs and lived with a guy named Bart Wolfe at Coronado Heights trailer park. He's that fellow that got shot at the Indian ruins a while back." Romero looked satisfied with his recitation and seemed to be waiting for a compliment from the sheriff.

"The ME give you any idea of the time lapses between murders?" Medrano asked.

"Roughly. First victim died in December, number two in January, three and four around mid-April and June. The dates pretty much coincide with when they were reported missing.

"Anna Mali, the fifth victim, seems to be a random killing, not connected to these. Santa Fe PD has a suspect—a transient. Only been in town a few months. Rules him out on the other murders."

Medrano thumbed through the photographs. "The victims have anything in common—tall, thin, blond, hookers, anything?"

"Only that they're between twenty and thirty. Small, attractive women. Liked to party and spent a lot of their free time at the bar in Madrid."

"They were all on the petite side," Jemimah chimed in. She was feeling left out of the conversation.

Medrano walked over to the thermostat. "Kind of warm in here, don't you think?" he said, twisting the dial. "The media's busting with speculation, trying to incite the public, scaring them into believing a madman's on the loose. Damn phones won't stop ringing."

Romero loosened his tie. "I hear you. My office is fielding calls right and left. Once Charlie Cooper's body was found, we figured we had our killer. We were ready to close the case. But it turns out Charlie's blood had a high concentration of drugs and alcohol. It's likely he was murdered."

Jemimah shot Romero a 'get to the point' look.

"So the killer is still on the loose?" Medrano frowned. "I can't go into re-election with this case hanging over my head like that. Not going to bode well with the media."

"Jemimah's been working non-stop on this case," Romero offered. He evidently felt she needed defending, which irritated the hell out of her, but she held her peace. "I'll let her fill you in on what she's come up with."

"I've spent a lot of time gathering material on this case," Jemimah said. "This is not your typical 'mad-dog killer who's scouring the streets looking for victims.' These seem to be specific killings."

"Specific, rather than random. What makes you think that?" Medrano interrupted.

"I'm thinking 'wrong place, wrong time' type of murders. All these women had been out with Charlie Cooper at one time or another, probably slept with him, and they all ended up dead. Why? Did he kill them? Probably not," she said.

"That sounds pretty speculative, Miss Hodge. How do we know he wasn't stalking them, looking for the right opportunity to kill them?" The Sheriff's manner was impatient.

Jemimah re-crossed her legs. "Well, I don't think he was capable of killing these women. He just doesn't fit the profile."

"Cooper's that fellow that everyone thought committed suicide out at the cabin in the Sandias. Now you're telling me we've got another murder on our hands?" The Sheriff shook his head.

"Looks that way, yes. When I met with the ME last week, he was leaning toward the suicide theory, but I remembered someone mentioning that Charlie was left-handed. The gun was in his right hand when he was found," Jemimah said.

"And that proves what?" The Sheriff said.

"So they did more testing and determined that the traces of gunpowder residue on his hand were minimal. There should have been more." Jemimah was beginning to get flustered.

"More residue? Many cases are solved with minimal gunpowder residue. It doesn't take much. The guy might have just offed himself. People do that." Medrano drummed his fingers on the table. "Let's leave the technicalities to the forensics squad."

"I think someone probably shot him then put the gun in his hand to make it look like a suicide," Jemimah said.

Romero raised his eyebrows. This was all new to him. She looked back at him, trying not to look too smug.

"It's all in that report I just handed you, Rick," she said. "Sorry. We didn't have a chance to talk about it before."

The temperature in the room was growing warmer by the minute. Jemimah wondered if Medrano had turned the thermostat down or up. Maybe she was feeling intimidated by his questions. She fanned the lapels of her blouse.

"Dr. Hodge seems to think this is the work of a psychotic killer," Rick Romero said. "Someone who had contact not only with Cooper but with each of the victims."

She thought about blowing him a kiss, so grateful was she that he was siding with her.

"Where are you going with this, Miss Hodge?" Sheriff Medrano interrupted her thoughts. "Quite frankly I'm going to need a little more convincing. After all, you are the new kid on the block. I can buy speculation seven days a week for a dollar a pound."

Jemimah pushed her chair back, almost knocking it over. She grabbed her shoulder bag and exited.

40

Sheriff Medrano threw his hands up. "Jeezus, did I say something?" By the time Lieutenant Romero reached the door, Jemimah was running down the hallway. She almost knocked a janitor over as she lunged toward the bathroom. She leaned over the sink, wet a towel and wiped her eyes. She took a few deep breaths to calm herself down before re-entering the hallway. Romero was standing by the water fountain. He put a hand on her shoulder.

"Hey, Jem. What's the matter? You all right?"

"That condescending son of a bitch. Such a damn know-it-all. He was belittling everything I said. And what's this 'Miss Hodge' bullshit? Maybe I should have brought my diplomas with me."

"That's just the way he is. Always tries to rattle everyone's cage. We just let it slide off our backs. He meant nothing by it, Jem. Maybe I should have warned you, but I figured you had already picked up on that. Come on, let's get back in there and finish this meeting off."

Jemimah was a little embarrassed. Romero kept his hand lightly touching the small of her back as they walked back into the office. Sheriff Medrano was on the phone. He motioned them to sit.

Jemimah spoke first. "I'm sorry, Sheriff. This case seems to have made me a little emotional. Where were we?"

"You were about to tell us where you're going with these findings of yours," he said.

She cleared her throat. "I've narrowed it down to one suspect, who wasn't on the original list. Cooper had an on again-off again live-in girlfriend for over a year. I spoke to the barmaid and the bartender at the Madrid bar. According to them, Brenda Mason was insanely jealous. Every time Cooper even looked at another woman, she made a scene and stomped out, madder than hell. Charlie would hang around, keep drinking and dancing, and leave with the new woman. Brenda tended to show up at closing time, subdued and apologetic, looking for Charlie."

Medrano flipped through the file. He made a note on his yellow pad and looked at Jemimah. "How do the murdered women fit into this?"

"These women were all Charlie's type. Small-boned, petite, and ready to get it on. Brenda fits in the looks category, but she's strong and athletic, works out at a local gym, runs marathons and is in better shape than most men."

Romero sat up. "I tracked down one woman who was at the ranch when Anaya went out to talk to Charlie about some loose cattle. She decided she didn't want to miss her class at the Community College and got a ride back with Anaya—you know how horny he is."

Medrano laughed. "I've called that old buzzard to task a couple of times. He's going to get us into a discrimination suit yet."

Romero walked over to the Formica sideboard and refilled his coffee cup. "Tiny woman with big brown eyes and a shapely figure. Good things come in small packages."

Romero returned to the table, sat down and reached across Jemimah for the sugar and cream, his arm brushing hers. She picked up the creamer and banged it down in front of him, sloshing some of it onto the table. It was clear to her why these two got along so well. She clenched her teeth and spoke slowly.

"Something like that. The point is, it wouldn't take much to drug these women, carry them out to the barn, kill them and drag them down into the tunnel."

"Charlie could have easily done that," Romero said.

"Yes, but Charlie was an easy-going, lovable druggie," she said. "He was really only interested in the sex, and he could always find another woman ready to get it on at the drop of a hat."

"So where does that leave us?" said the Sheriff, visibly annoyed at the tit-for-tat between these two.

"The girlfriend, Brenda," Jemimah said.

Romero looked at the Sheriff. "Sounds plausible to me."

"You've almost convinced me," Sheriff Medrano admitted.

Jemimah pushed on. She wanted to get this over with. "I interviewed a couple of guys at the bar who said Charlie was bragging about pulling off a big deal and heading down to Mexico. Alone. Wanted to spend his time drinking, fishing, and courting senoritas."

"So how did Brenda get the women into the barn?" Romero asked. "Force them at gun point or what?"

"No, I figure she drugged the bottle of whiskey that Charlie always kept around with a slow-acting date rape drug, maybe Burundang or Ketamine—"

"Special K," Romero supplied.

"You would probably know," Jemimah said. "In the cupboard you found a bottle that was sent off to be tested. The remaining whiskey had an odd smell to it. The ME has sent off tissue samples to see if a drug screen can be run on them. That's still possible even where there's decomposition.

"If Charlie and a woman were unconscious on the bed, Brenda could have carried the woman out to the barn. There was an old red Radio Flyer wagon that could have also been used to transport bodies. It's being tested for blood. Once she got the victim into the barn, she could have slit her throat, dragged the body on a plastic tarp for a short distance down the ramp and left her stashed in the tunnel. I don't think she ever intended to move the bodies. That's why she shot McCabe, because he was getting too close. He was bound to find the shaft and the bodies, particularly if sophisticated geological probing tests were conducted beforehand."

Rick admired Jemimah's tenacity. Medrano was quiet, a sure sign that he was listening to every word. He said, "So she knew that, in the natural course of events, the bodies would be found; that's why she wanted to get rid of McCabe."

"Exactly," Jemimah said.

"All right, Lieutenant." Medrano stood up "Seems like the ball's in our court now. Let's figure out where we want to go from here."

"I'll get right on it," Romero said. "Jemimah's looking into Brenda Mason's background. She needs to make a trip to Denver to interview a psychiatrist there. Once she's back with her findings, we can set up the arrest warrants. When we get our sights on Mason, we'll bring her in for questioning."

"Here's the approval form for that Colorado trip, Doctor Hodge. Get it over to accounting and they'll run it through. Good work. Now get out of here, both of you."

Jemimah shook his hand firmly. She knew their next meeting wouldn't be as unnerving as this one.

41

The squad room at the substation was half the size of the two offices. There was a white melamine table in the center, the kind used at flea markets and garage sales, six metal folding chairs around it. Romero, Martinez and Chacon were comparing notes on the case. They had foam coffee cups in front of them. A box of donuts sat next to the yellow pads, pens and clipboards.

"Okay," Romero said. "Here's where we stand. According to ballistics, the bullet that killed Charlie Cooper and the one that injured McCabe were the same, a Glock automatic. Rifling characteristics were identical. So either Cooper fired it or someone else had access to it."

They browsed through photos of the crime scene. Four women each with their throats cut. Chacon felt uncomfortable reviewing the photos. It was enough to have been in attendance at the autopsies. "The killer took the time to pose each one," Romero said, "and put a tag around her neck with the words BITCH, WHORE, WHITE TRASH and LOSER. Don't remember ever seeing that in past cases. That's a fact we haven't released to the media."

Martinez was the rookie detective, still feeling his way around crime scenes. "Look at this victim. Still has her earrings and necklace on. Spooky."

Romero pushed a couple more photos toward the two detectives. "Other than at the throat, not much evidence of assault. Same weapon—a medium-sized butcher knife with a narrow blade—found at the scene. Kept sharp, maybe for butchering beef or deer. Probably from the ranch house. We found a set of old knives that the owner said were in a kitchen drawer when he moved into the property. They all have similar handles."

"How about the guy who owns the ruins?" asked Chacon, reaching for a donut. The powdered sugar spilled on his tie. He ceremoniously wiped it off with a napkin.

"McCabe told me he didn't know the underground shaft existed," Romero said. "They weren't at that advanced stage of exploration. He and his archaeological crew hadn't done much more than surface digging—arrowheads, beads and such."

"You think he's telling the truth?" asked Chacon, as he unrolled yet another Tootsie Roll. "I noticed he didn't hang around the site too long after the bodies were taken out. Seemed like he was anxious to get out of there."

"Crisssake, he's an ex-sheriff," Romero said. "And a long-time friend of Medrano's to boot."

"Ex-cop, you say? Like they never killed anyone except in the line of duty? Maybe that's why he's not a working cop anymore. Did you ever look into his record?" Chacon continued to dig at Romero.

"I think it was as much of a shock to him as it was to us. And remember, there's been no active exploration at those ruins since the 1950s. And even then it was superficial; they didn't have the technology that exists now. McCabe planned on conducting serious archaeological studies later this summer. For your information," Romero added, "McCabe has an impeccable record. Heroic, for that matter. Let's move on, here."

"So spell it out for us," said Martinez. "We got a suspect?"

"Cooper's girlfriend is our main suspect," Romero said. "We figure she not only killed the women, but also did in Cooper."

"I don't see anything in the file that points directly to her," Chacon said. "There's no indication that she was anywhere near him when he was killed."

"Jemimah Hodge, the department's Forensic Psychologist, is in Denver following up on a lead on the girlfriend," Romero said. "As soon as she gets back, I'll fill you in. Until then, I think we need to pursue any pending tips, just in case there are loose threads."

"Sounds like we're moving full speed ahead," said Chacon. "But it's going to take a little more than our blond coworker's theories to convince me. She a detective, or what?"

Romero let Chacon's remark slide by him. Chacon continued on. "Hey, we know you're sweet on her, Amigo, but from where I sit, we need a lot more than just sheer conjecture to solve this crime."

Romero stood up and removed his jacket. It was too warm a day to be in full uniform. "Don't be such an asshole, Arty Boy. You're just pissed because she's the only one around here with answers. I don't see you offering any earth-shattering solutions." He sat back down and shuffled papers from the folder.

Chacon prodded on. "The jury's still out on that. We need some hard evidence. Don't see much of it in the file."

Martinez chimed in. "All right you guys. Settle down. I see where Rick's going with this. We have to proceed with caution and not put all our eggs in one basket. Much of the circumstantial evidence is pointing to the girlfriend. Who else could it be? She had daily access to him."

"You both know how easily coincidence can be explained away," said Romero. "So we need to continue following up on any tips that come in, no matter how far-fetched. When Dr. Hodge returns, I'm sure she'll have it all lined up for us."

"Well, Lieutenant. Let's hope your pretty little girlfriend can come up with the goods. Don't want to ruin your chances of getting her in the sack," Chacon chortled and snuffed his cigarette out in his coffee cup.

Chacon didn't see the right jab coming at his face.

42

Jemimah parked her car in the short-term lot at the airport in Albuquerque. She picked up her ticket and boarding pass at the counter and boarded the Southwest Airlines flight, which lasted seventy-five minutes. Arriving in Denver, she rented a car and drove north on Interstate 70 toward Grape Street. She turned into the visitors' lot and walked up the brick pathway toward the air-conditioned lobby. The hospital grounds were pristine, the lawn trimmed short. Rows and rows of perennials ran along the edge of the sidewalk. Not a one was wilted.

As she entered the building, a security guard directed her to the receptionist, a pleasant woman who said Dr. Garland would be with her shortly. Five minutes later a man in a white coat walked toward her.

"I'm Dr. Garland." He gave Jem a firm handshake and directed her to his office. She sat in the brown leather chair facing him. Framed diplomas and certificates lined the walls. A faux Ficus tree in a large green pot occupied one corner. Even in this room, a strong antiseptic smell permeated the air.

"My name is Jemimah Hodge." She handed him her card. "Thank you for seeing me on such short notice."

Dr. Garland was light-haired, tanned, and muscular—a poster boy for fitness. His voice was soothing, like a psychiatrist should be, she thought.

He took a chair behind his desk and propped his feet on top. "Dr. Hodge, you said you wanted to talk about Brenda Mason?"

"Yes," she said. I'm a forensic psychologist working on a case with the Santa Fe County Sheriff's Department in New Mexico."

"And how does that concern Brenda?" He thumbed through a manila folder on his desk as if he knew he was not going to get a specific answer.

"We're investigating the disappearance of a number of women around Santa Fe. Brenda is a person of interest. I'm looking into her background to determine if we might need to consider her a suspect at this time. I'm primarily interested in the reasons you saw her as an inpatient."

"I've gone over her file to refresh my memory. Brenda attempted to assault a woman sitting in a restaurant with her former boyfriend. I believe she was arrested for disorderly conduct and spent a few days in jail before being arraigned. The judge sentenced her to either ninety days at our facility or six months in jail." His glasses kept sliding down his nose as he talked. "As you know, she opted to spend the three months with us."

"What can you tell me about her without breaching your doctor-patient relationship?" Jemimah asked.

He peered at her through his horn-rimmed glasses. The furrows on his forehead deepened. He well knew the type of person Brenda was. She was a Class A sociopath. His dilemma was how to respond to Jemimah's questions without putting the hospital in jeopardy.

"Not a lot I can say, you understand. But I can point you toward the boyfriend. He's a local fellow, and perhaps he'd be willing to speak with you." He removed his glasses, adjusted the nosepiece, and put them back on. "Brenda was a textbook case with a number of issues. As you're aware, those cases follow an established pattern." He spoke generically, but Jemimah realized he was giving her the straight info on Brenda.

"She refuses to take any blame for a particular incident or for many other events in her life. If a suitor breaks up with her, she may stalk him, turning up at his place of employment, sporting events, restaurants. If he appears in public with a girl, whether she is a girlfriend or merely an associate from work, she accosts them and creates a scene. She will declare she loves him and can't understand why they broke up, conduct which under ordinary circumstances might be considered shameful."

"I see." Jemimah sensed that Dr. Garland was going to talk—despite his protests about not being able to offer much—as he suddenly lapsed into calling his theoretical patient by name.

The doctor swung his chair around and put his feet down. He reached into a drawer, pulled out a spritzer bottle and a tissue and proceeded to clean his glasses. Carefully and meticulously, he weighed each word as he spoke.

"Brenda was completely oblivious to the breakup. We often discussed her tendency to deny the obvious. Quite frankly, it's my opinion she suffered from a form of paranoid attachment syndrome. I'm sure you're familiar with that—an individual's incapacity to distinguish between someone who could actually care for them and someone who they think will care for them."

"Was she on any medication while she was a patient?" Jemimah asked.

He walked toward the window, his hands clasped behind his back. "We tried various medications, Novoclopamine for one. I've had great success with patients suffering from psychotic episodes, which Brenda had exhibited. But she was a difficult case. Quite honestly I couldn't tell if she was really making progress or just play-acting. By the time she left here, she had turned into a model patient. She showed up for her scheduled appointments, participated in group therapy. My staff decided she was ready to move on. They had far more exposure to her than I did, and made the ultimate recommendations that she was capable of returning to society."

"Do you have any record of her family?" Jemimah said.

"She spoke very little about her parents." He sat down again and thumbed through the file. "It says here they were divorced. The mother remarried a couple of times and had another daughter. For years, Brenda had been in and out of psychiatric hospitals in California and more recently here in Colorado. As a child, she craved attention, good or bad. After her mother divorced her father, she remarried a man with a son about Brenda's age. Brenda became infatuated with him, believed he loved her, and after her mother divorced again, Brenda was devastated, more at the loss of her step-brother than anything else. She began to exhibit symptoms of severe depression and periodically landed in the hospital for treatment.

"That's about all we know. Brenda was narcissistic to a great degree, but could easily come off as thoughtful and caring. Nonetheless, I detected a heart of pure stone."

"Did she say where she was going once she was released?" Jemimah was scribbling notes as fast as she could. This guy was a gold mine of information. She no longer feared the whole trip might turn out to be a wild goose chase.

"Well, as I recall, she mentioned New Mexico," he said. "Brenda was very intelligent. She scored high on all the standard tests. In addition, she exhibited all the classic traits of an addict—drank, smoked, did crystal meth, anything and everything. But she had the uncanny ability to function as though she was clean. It was the kind of behavior researchers love to write about."

He looked up as the grandfather clock in the corner chimed eleven. Jemimah was surprised that the morning had progressed so rapidly.

"Just a few more questions, Doctor. What about violence, did she have any additional episodes after she came here?"

"Not that I witnessed. The meds probably helped with that. But there's no doubt in my mind she was capable of it. She either kept it in check or never encountered an occasion where she felt it was necessary. She was also acutely aware that misbehavior would extend her sentence."

"Have you heard from her at all?" she said.

"No, I haven't. If you wait here a few minutes, I'll get the boyfriend's number for you." He returned to his desk, scribbled on a piece of paper and handed it to her.

Jemimah thanked him and walked out to her car. She dialed Jimmy Fernando's number and made an appointment to see him later in the day. She had a few hours to kill, so she called Robin Pierce, an old college roommate, who was now a curator at the Denver Art Museum. They met for lunch in the Museum's restaurant.

43

Jimmy Fernando was Brenda's ex-boyfriend. He agreed to talk to Jemimah about Brenda and gave her directions to his place.

Jemimah drove up I-25 and turned onto Cherry Creek, where side-by-side Victorian brick houses were lined up in a neat row. She turned at Third Avenue, found the black mailbox with the numbers 1028, and turned into the driveway. The building was next to the Botanical Gardens in the Cherry Creek neighborhood, in the center of the ebb and flow of the mile-high city at the foot of the Rocky Mountains.

Jimmy Fernando buzzed Jemimah in on the first ring of the doorbell. She walked up the steps to door number three where he stood and invited her into the living room. Jimmy was a sheet metal fabricator for a company on the outskirts of Denver, a robust, cheerful guy with hazel green eyes that had a mischievous glint. He was of medium height, maybe five-eight or so, with mostly brown hair. He must have been over thirty, but the heavily jelled blond streaks in his hair made him appear much younger. His arms were covered with tribal tattoos. His smile revealed a chipped front tooth.

The place was neat as a pin, much like he was. He wore a crisp white shirt, tan Dockers, and black cordovan loafers—hardly his work clothes. He motioned her over to the couch and offered coffee. From his living room you could see spectacular views of the mountains and the downtown Denver skyline.

"Mr. Fernando," Jemimah said. "Thank you for agreeing to talk to me."

"Jimmy," he said. "There's probably not much I can tell you. I haven't seen Brenda for over two years now."

"Tell me a little about your relationship," she said.

"Well, when I first met Brenda, I thought she was 'the one.' Smart, sweet, thoughtful, caring and a lot of fun to be around. We did everything together. About six months into the relationship, I noticed she was drinking a lot more, always wanting to go out and party, you know. Hey, I like to party as much as the next guy," he laughed, "but I also have to get up in the morning and go to work."

"Were you living together at the time?" she said.

"Yeah, we pretty much moved in together right away. I can see now that it wasn't such a good idea. Our lifestyles were just too different. I wanted to settle down, she didn't."

"How long were you together?"

"Oh, I don't know, maybe less than a year. By that time she had become insanely jealous, giving me the third degree about everything I did, anyone I talked to. I had to constantly assure her that I loved her. She called me up at work just to ask if I loved her that particular day. At first I was flattered, but then it started to get a little over the top. I told her it wasn't going to work out between us and she left. I think she rented an apartment somewhere in the Heights."

"Did she have family in Denver?"

"No, she rarely mentioned family," he said. "I think her parents might have been divorced, but she never went into detail." He stirred cream and two sugars into his coffee. Jemimah smiled. He seemed like a pretty nice guy to be hooked up with someone as unpredictable as Brenda.

"So what happened after you broke up?"

"I didn't see her for about two months and then she started showing up wherever I happened to be. Starbucks, lunch, the gym. She would just smile and wave. One night I was in a restaurant with Paula, a really nice woman I was thinking about starting up a relationship with. Brenda came out of nowhere, pulled up a chair and sat down. It was awkward. She introduced herself as my girlfriend and motioned to the waiter for a drink. Embarrassed, Paula excused herself and went to the powder room. I told Brenda she had to leave. She kept saying, 'Why, Jimmy, why? We can work this out. Give me another chance.' I promised I would call her, but I never did."

"So what happened after that?" asked Jemimah.

"Brenda gets up to leave. Paula comes back and sits down. Brenda puts her hand on Paula's wrist and starts screaming obscenities at her, calling her a slut. Then she grabs a steak knife from the table and lunges at her, hollering, 'I'll slit your throat, bitch.' It took me and two of the waiters to bring her down. She didn't stop screaming the entire time. The police came, arrested her, and I haven't seen her since. I heard the Judge sentenced her to a loony bin somewhere in Colorado."

"Did you press charges?" Jemimah could tell the conversation was difficult for him.

"No, but Paula did. She went down to the police station and filed a complaint. A couple of the waiters testified at the hearing. Lucky for me, I didn't have to go to court."

"What happened to Paula? Did Brenda frighten her away?"

"I never thought about that, but she probably did. We never had another date after that. I called her a couple of times but could never reach her. Can't hardly blame her. Seems like she just dropped out of sight. Who knows, maybe she figured I was some kind of freak and didn't want anything to do with me."

Jemimah thought to herself that there might be more to it than that, but didn't want to open up a can of worms with nothing more than a gut feeling about what might have really happened to Paula.

"Thank you, Jimmy," she said. You've been a great help."

"No problem," he said, showing her to the door.

44

Jemimah drove down the six-lane Interstate 70 in Denver—more traffic than in both Santa Fe and Albuquerque combined. She was glad she lived in Two-Main-Road Santa Fe, with no possibility of a freeway ever being built near it. Her exit came up quickly and she found the hotel with ease.

She sat on the bed in Room 118 of Denver's historic Curtis Hotel, a large eclectic Victorian built in the 1800s. The hotel was small by Santa Fe standards, with only six stories and 150 rooms. But this wasn't a pleasure trip. She preferred to stay in a central location where she could accomplish what she set out to do and return home.

Her room overlooked a pedestrian park with sandstone sidewalks. The trolley clanked noisily toward the station on the next block. It was early in the evening and a steady rain pelted her window. She didn't feel much like sitting alone in the restaurant, so she decided to order from room service. She intended to catch a flight back to Albuquerque around seven the next morning.

She called Rick and told him what she had discovered about Brenda. There was no doubt in her mind that Brenda had not only killed each of the women in a jealous rage, but Charlie, too. Their conversation made her more determined than ever to have Brenda picked up for questioning. Romero told her that when she returned to Santa Fe, they would set up surveillance at her residence and at the bar in Madrid. Jemimah told Rick of her theory that Jimmy Fernando's new girlfriend had probably met the same fate as the murdered women in Santa Fe. She would leave it to Rick to pursue that avenue with the Colorado State Police when the time came.

She reached over and set the alarm clock. Fifteen minutes later she was cozying up to the blankets. She could hear her phone ringing somewhere in the room. *Where was it?* She emptied her purse as it continued to ring. She finally retrieved it from the zipped pocket of her suitcase. Whitney's name flashed across its face.

"Hello, Whitney. Long time no hear," she said, yawning.

"Been waiting for you to return my call, Jem," he drawled. "Too busy these days?"

"I've meant to get back to you. Right now I'm in Denver. Can this wait?" It was an effort to keep the annoyance out of her voice.

"You got a second?" he said.

"Sure," she gave in. "But make it short."

"You know that cold case I was asking for your opinion on?"

"The woman in the red corvette, yes, I do." Jemimah didn't think this was something that couldn't wait.

"Listen, I've been reviewing the file. Spoke to a few of the witnesses, and I'm thinking it's not worth pursuing. Probably cost the taxpayers a whole bunch of money and then turn out to be a dead end."

Jemimah was surprised. She could feel the pitch of her voice rising. "Not worth pursuing? A woman's dead under suspicious circumstances. It sounded like a cover-up to me."

"I just said I did some investigating into the circumstances, and I'm reclosing the file," he said.

"Are you sure? I ..." Jemimah stammered.

"Case closed, Jemimah," he said abruptly. "Already filed away."

"Your call, Whitney." She wasn't ready to debate the point.

His tone of voice changed to one dripping with honey. "So what you doing this Friday. Want to have dinner?"

"No thanks. I'm pretty involved in this case. I'll probably be doing a surveillance that night," she said.

"My, my. Aren't we moving up the ladder. Rain check?"

"I'll think about it and let you know," she said.

"Getting sweet on the Lieutenant, are we?"

"Put a sock in it, Whitney," she said, annoyed.

"Pleasant dreams, Jem." He hung up.

Jemimah thought about the case Whitney had asked her opinion on. Even a cursory examination pointed to a blue wall erected around it. She was sure there was a lot more to it than Whitney was letting on. Maybe he had just used the case as an excuse to get closer to her and then realized she had read more into it than he expected.

Or maybe he had a deeper, darker involvement.

45

On Saturday, Rick Romero decided he needed a break. He had been working non-stop on his caseload. A drive south on Highway 14 might help him develop a new perspective on things. He loved the hilly terrain of the Cerrillos area. It encompassed elements of wonder and beauty, ever-changing on the horizon. About fifteen miles out, he drove up to Sandia Crest, the highest point of the Sandia mountain range, which stretched farther south to surround the Albuquerque landscape.

Romero parked his car, walked a short distance, and sat on a rocky escarpment to look out on the vast expanse. The sky was dark and cloudy, threatening a rainstorm. But it didn't matter to him. A series of lightning bolts generated a dazzling light show over the Sandias. A sense of peace and stillness permeated his entire being.

In the 1950s, an airliner had crashed at the top of the highest peak of the Sandias. There were no survivors, and because of the difficulty in reaching the plane, only those items that could be recovered were brought down the mountain. Some twenty years later as a teenager, Romero climbed the face of the mountain with his father, curious to see the wreckage eleven thousand feet up. Each time he drove on I-25, he could still see the glint of the sun reflecting off the remaining metal skeleton of the plane.

It had been a while since Romero had taken the opportunity to relax with nature. The surrounding fields below were covered with purple and yellow wildflowers, in contrast to the carpets of cholla cactus growing next to the highway. There was a lot he had to think about. For months he'd been hoping he and Jemimah could embark on a romantic relationship, but that wasn't working out. As a police officer, long term relationships scared the crap out of him. Were he to be killed on duty, the ones he left behind would suffer. But then again, up to this point he really hadn't met anyone he wanted to become deeply involved with.

These rare moments of relaxation always brought up the past for Romero. As a young man he didn't want to be Spanish—his parents' culture. He endured years of teasing and name-calling for his home-cut hair and for the way he and his group of friends butchered the English language. By the time he graduated from high school, Romero had honed his language skills and learned to speak English without a hint of an accent.

He spent the next couple of hours sitting on the side of the mountain gazing out over the landscape. Another round of lightning made its way through the sky, pausing for a millisecond and then erupting again. From force of habit he counted to seven and, as if on cue, the clap of thunder reverberated all around him. He smiled as he thought about the childhood game his mother had introduced to him on rainy days. Years later he'd come to find out that it wasn't an old wives' tale.

The rain began as a slight drizzle, small droplets refreshing his face. By the time he decided to walk back to his car, he was drenched. He laughed, recalling the many times his grandmother chided him for not having enough sense to come in out of the rain.

46

Brenda Mason resided in a small two-bedroom house on a side street a few blocks from downtown Santa Fe. She rented a room from Sonja Swentzel, a forty-something woman who remained stuck in the sixties. Sonja dressed in long cotton broom-skirts and puff-sleeved lace tops, with rows of colored corn necklaces and faux turquoise beads around her neck. She was pale-eyed and pale-complexioned, with brown hair down to her waist. Unlike Brenda, who was always high, Sonja was a whiny, depressing person. She had glommed on to every assistance program offered by Santa Fe County. Brenda saw her as a malingerer who spent most of her time thinking of ways to scam the State, the County or the City, to talk them into paying for more of her expenses and those of her now full-grown illegitimate son. She had racked up over a quarter of a million dollars in assistance since he was born twenty-five years earlier, and some poor fool she'd selected as a sperm donor was now up to his ass in debt to the State for all those years of back child support she claimed he never paid.

Sonja might be an opportunist, but she was no dummy. She had just never taken advantage of her college education. Instead of using her Master's degree, she preferred to be on the dole. The City paid the rent on her house, and she rented part of it to Brenda, who took her time paying the rent. Brenda knew it annoyed Sonja that she only stayed there when it was convenient, spending the remainder of the time with Charlie or some other temporary boyfriend.

Brenda pulled into Sonja's driveway. She reached over to the back seat, grabbed Charlie's backpack and sauntered up the brick sidewalk. The small adobe house was typical of the area, except that the front door was painted bright yellow—Sonja's idea of drawing the sun's energy. Brenda

157

turned the key and opened the door. She was glad Sonja wasn't home. She went into the bathroom, stripped off her clothes, and drew a bath. As she toweled off, she debated whether to stay home or go out for drinks. On the way home, Brenda stopped at a trendy shop on the plaza and bought herself a skirt, top and a pair of sandals. In the bedroom, she took the new outfit out of the shopping bag and got dressed.

She reached into Charlie's backpack, grabbed a handful of bills and put them in an envelope for Sonja with a note stating that she intended to move at the end of the month. She emptied the contents of the backpack on the bed, stuffed the bills into a small overnight satchel and hid it under a stack of junk in the closet.

Brenda stood in front of the full-length mirror. *Killer extraordinaire*, she thought as she checked her makeup. She sat down at her computer, logged on to the local newspaper site and scanned the local news. She erupted into raucous laughter as she read the front page headline about four women found dead in Santa Fe County. Could there possibly be a connection to the recent shootings, the reporter asked the Police captain. "Shit, yeah," Brenda raised her arm to mimic the pull of a train whistle. "Every one of these bitches slept with Charlie. That's your connection, asshole."

When she was twenty-two, a psychiatrist had told her the psychotic episodes would return unless she stayed on the meds. He prescribed Xyprexa and Haldol and told her to see him in a month, but she never kept the appointment; she could buy all the drugs she needed on the street. She moved to Colorado and found a job and an apartment in Denver. Things progressed smoothly until the breakup with Jimmy Fernando. To get even with Jimmy for dumping her, she killed his new girlfriend. That would fix *his* ass. She packed up all her stuff and moved to New Mexico. When she met Charlie, everything was fine until she told him she was leaving. She had been sure that he would profess his love and beg her to stay. Instead he had told her not to let the door kick her in the ass on the way out.

After the breakup with Charlie, Brenda began parking her car a short distance from the ranch. When she saw the lights go out, she sneaked in through the sunroom door, which Charlie never locked. She had previously drugged the bottle of whiskey he kept in the cupboard. When he and his date had passed out, she lifted the woman onto the little red wagon the old lady who owned the ranch had used for carrying firewood. In the barn, she placed the limp body on the plastic tarp, slit its throat and dragged it down the ramp to the tunnel. Charlie woke up the next morning thinking the woman had left in the middle of the night.

Brenda had discovered the entrance to the tunnel quite by accident while scouring the barn for Charlie's stash of grass. She spotted a piece of old canvas sheeting under a layer of dirt and figured it might be covering a hiding place. Lifting the edge of the frayed tarp exposed a metal grate over what appeared to be a tunnel. Shining a flashlight ahead of her, she followed the shaft for a thousand feet—she couldn't tell exactly how far—until it ended at a four-rung ladder. She climbed up the ladder but had a hard time dislodging the boulder over the exit. Finally it gave. Emerging from the other end of the tunnel, she was momentarily disoriented. What a surprise to find herself at the cave at Medicine Rock. From where she was standing, she could see all the way to the barn. Holy shit.

When Brenda killed the first woman, she decided to stash the body in the shaft until she could drag it over and dump it in the old well some distance behind the barn. But she never had that chance. Besides, it looked like nobody had ever been in the tunnel, not even Charlie, and it pleased her that she had found the perfect hiding place.

Initially there was only going to be one victim before Brenda attempted to get Charlie back in her life, but that asshole was never satisfied. He had to have every woman. At least once every couple of weeks he brought a new someone home to the ranch. There were probably more that Brenda didn't know about, but she couldn't keep track of him twenty four-seven, however hard she tried.

Brenda stared at herself in the mirror, deep in thought. *I'm Scot free; the cops are focusing on Charlie.* Right now she was looking forward to having a drink at the bar in Madrid and getting on with life. That fifty grand was going to make life much, much easier.

47

At the Mine Shaft Tavern in Madrid Brenda sat on a barstool in front of the forty-foot wooden bar. The place was just dark enough. Neon signs illuminated the backdrop of the bar. The place was weighted with stale cigarette smoke, western memorabilia and cowboy kitsch. A pool table sat in the center of the back room, cue sticks lined up against the wall. The bartender was a stocky hunk of a man with long brown hair grown out of control. It was Margarita hour. Brenda motioned to him, and he set a drink in front of her.

She eyed her reflection in the mirror behind the bar. She had been a patron here ever since moving from Colorado. These were her type of people: rowdy, nonconformist, but all hard-drinking bar-friendly folks. She never fit into the haughty Santa Fe night scene. It was too phony for her. Everything was just fine here. She was dressed in a short skirt, a black Lycra top and leather boots, all of which accentuated her well-toned physique. There was no question that she was fit and strong. A group of regulars hunched over their drinks, cigarette ashes dropping casually to the floor as they discussed football, the economy, and women in general.

Jemimah drove into the Tavern parking lot. She was there to meet Tim McCabe. She spotted his familiar silver Hummer rumbling toward the parking lot. She placed her notes back in her briefcase and stepped out of the car. It was seven o'clock, but the sun was taking its time slipping behind the mountain. She waved at McCabe. They walked into the bar together, hoping to encounter Brenda in her element. Julie the barmaid came over to greet them and directed them to a corner table where they could observe people coming and going. Jemimah introduced herself and McCabe and they both ordered Budweiser on tap.

As the bartender poured beer into glass mugs and slid them across the bar to Julie, Brenda motioned for a refill on her rum and Coke. Julie carried the tray to McCabe and Jemimah and placed the beer on their table. She leaned over to hand them napkins.

"She's here," she said to Jemimah. I'll point her out to you.

Julie worked her way across the room over to Brenda, wiping tables in her path. She motioned to Jemimah, then picked up Brenda's empty glass, took it behind the bar and placed it in a plastic bag. Oblivious, the bartender continued to mix drinks and unpack cases of liquor. Julie handed the bagged glass with Brenda's fingerprints to Jemimah. McCabe would deliver it to the Forensics lab.

48

Brenda confronted Julie in the bathroom.

"Who was that couple you were so chummy with, Julie?" she said.

"Which couple you talking about?" Julie asked as she blew her hands dry.

"Don't play dumb. The ones you pointed mc out to."

Julie knew she was no match for Brenda, having been privy to her intimidating side on recent occasions.

"All right," she said. "I think she's some kind of investigator. I don't know him. Maybe he's a boyfriend."

"What's that got to do with me?" Brenda hissed.

"Nothing, I guess," Julie lied.

Brenda grabbed her arm and gave it a menacing twist. "C'mon, Julie. There's more to it than that."

Julie caved, fearing for her own safety. "The police are investigating Charlie's death. I guess they don't believe hc killed himself. Anyway, Brenda, I have to get back to the bar. I've been in here way too long. You know what an asshole the boss can be."

Brenda checked her makeup in the mirror and dismissed her with a wave of her hand. "Yeah, do that."

Julie returned to the floor. McCabe and Jemimah were just leaving. She knew Brenda would hurt her if she went out to talk to them, so she didn't.

Brenda watched as McCabe walked Jemimah out to her car. They stood a few minutes, deep in conversation. Brenda took a good look at Jemimah's car as it pulled out of the parking lot. Brenda got into her car and followed several car lengths behind Jemimah. McCabe was already out of sight down the highway.

Jemimah turned right on the dirt road leading to her ranch house, triggering the security lights. It had been a long day and she was looking forward to a hot bath. Brenda waited a distance behind and parked her car next to a grouping of boulders near the Garden of the Gods, a wind-sculpted rock formation stretching for miles along the side of the highway. Her vehicle would be obscured from view. She took a pistol from the glove compartment and tucked it in the waist of her skirt. Walking around in the dark didn't bother Brenda. Charlie used to tease her about being a cat.

Before she had left the bar, she had grabbed a couple of meat patties from the kitchen. Used to dealing with barking dogs, she cracked open two capsules of animal tranquilizer and blended them into the meat. Just in case there was a dog on the property, the fast-acting medicine would take them down quickly. She walked through the gate on Jemimah's property, creeping along the edge of the fence to where the security lights didn't extend.

Jemimah's dog tripped the light as it ambled toward Brenda, tail wagging but uncertain if she was friend or foe. Brenda threw the meat out toward the edge of the drive. The curious Border Collie crept under a bush next to the fence, gobbled the meat in one swallow and dropped in its tracks. Brenda waited until the light went out before she moved.

49

Jemimah walked out from the bathroom in a terry robe, a towel wrapped around her head. She felt refreshed. As she clicked on the television set to catch the late news before she called it a night, she looked around for her cell phone to call Rick and fill him in on the night's events. By now McCabe should have dropped the glass off at the forensics lab. There was a knock at the door. Jemimah smiled in anticipation. It was probably Rick, stopping in to say goodnight or, wishful thinking, even good morning. Just this afternoon she had decided it was time to drop the barriers between them. She pulled the towel off her head and tossed her phone on the couch.

Jemimah opened the door wide, intending to put her arms out and surprise him with an embrace. Brenda barged in and shoved her back into the living room. She had a pistol in her hand. Jemimah backed away.

"Sit down," Brenda ordered.

"Brenda, this is a mistake. What are you doing?" Jemimah said.

"Shut up. You think I had something to do with Charlie dying, don't you?" Brenda hissed.

"I don't have an opinion either way," Jemimah said, looking around for Molly. Where was that dog? "Please don't do this, Brenda. Turn yourself in. We'll get you help, I promise."

It was just a few minutes after midnight. Jemimah could see Brenda was a night owl. Wide awake. Alert. Nothing was going to get by her. She was holding the gun steady, pointed straight at Jemimah.

Brenda's pupils were dilated. Probably on drugs. Jemimah wracked her brain to figure out a way to overcome her. Otherwise she was certainly going to die.

"Come on, get up," Brenda ordered. "It's a little too comfy in here."

She pushed Jemimah into the kitchen and sat her on a stool in front of the granite-topped island. Brenda took out a roll of duct tape, pulled Jemimah's hands behind her and wrapped the tape securely around her hands, winding it through the backrest of the stool.

"There, that's better," Brenda said, sitting across the counter and placing the pistol in front of her. She opened one drawer then another before spotting the Maplewood cutlery set next to the stove. She picked out a knife and checked the blade. "I don't care for guns," she said. "They're so noisy. Me, I like quiet."

Jemimah started to say something.

"No, no, keep your mouth shut. I'm thinking. And remember, I prefer quiet," Brenda smirked.

* * *

It was getting late and Rick hadn't heard from Jemimah. She was supposed to call him when she and McCabe finished their surveillance at the bar in Madrid. McCabe had called in on his way to drop off the glass with the forensics lab. The tech was working late on the case and by now should have compared Brenda's prints on the glass to the bloody thumbprint they found on the lighter in Charlie's car.

Jeez. I'm acting like a mother hen, he thought—one of the many characteristics that got him in trouble with fiercely independent Jemimah. He decided it was too late to call her. He stretched out on his bed and turned off the lights. The illumination of the votive candle in front of his mother's shrine filled the room with a subtle glow. He rolled over on his side and was asleep in seconds. Tomorrow was going to be another long day.

50

Toward the early morning hours, Brenda dozed off just long enough to be refreshed. Jemimah had managed to put her head down on the counter, but hadn't been able to close her eyes. She spent the last five hours trying to figure out how she was going to get herself out of this mess. At seven o'clock, the phone rang. Probably Rick. Brenda looked up. "Don't answer that. Let it ring," she said.

"I'd better answer it, otherwise whoever is calling will know something's wrong," Jemimah said.

"All right, but no tricks." Brenda picked up the pistol and aimed it at Jemimah's head, holding the phone to her ear with her free hand.

"Hey, Jemimah. Everything all right?" Romero said in his most cheerful voice.

"Yeah, sure. How are you?" she said.

"I'm okay. But you sound a little distant," he said, figuring she was still pissed off at him for one thing or another.

"Sorry, I'm just a little unnerved. My dog Bobby got bitten by a coyote and I have to take him to the vet. You know how he pokes his nose where it doesn't belong. I'll probably be out of touch for the rest of the day. I'll get back with you later."

"Do you need some help with that?" he asked.

"Oh, thanks, but no. I'm sure Dr. Medrano can take care of it."

Brenda motioned for her to wrap it up.

"Listen, thanks again for calling. I have to go now."

Brenda checked the duct tape to make sure Jemimah couldn't pull loose. She looked around the house and walked to the window in the living room. The dog was still laid out near the fence, hidden from sight. It would be a while before the drugs wore off. She wouldn't have to worry about it until then. She would have just put a bullet through its head, but what was the point? The drugs had always worked on Charlie's dog whenever she needed to silence him.

* * *

Rick Romero called Tim McCabe and asked him how Jemimah had been feeling the night before.

"Fine," McCabe said. "We had one drink to keep up appearances while we were hanging out at the bar. She was in good spirits. Is something wrong?"

"Maybe. I just got off the phone with her and our conversation was pretty cryptic. Oh damn. Bobby ... Medrano ..." Romero said. "Shit!"

McCabe interjected, "That's the Sheriff's name."

"I think our girl just might be entertaining an unwanted guest. I'm just leaving the house. I'll swing by and pick you up. May need backup."

"I'll be waiting on the curb," said McCabe.

51

Brenda unceremoniously yanked the tape from Jemimah's hands, forced her to stand and pushed her through the kitchen and out the side door. They rushed across the gravel driveway to the pathway running parallel to the first mile of the Garden of the Gods. The morning sun was bright, harsh on unprotected eyes. The crisp air was fragrant with the carmine blooms of the orchid cactus lining the path. Mourning doves perched in a century old cottonwood tree. There wouldn't be much traffic out this early, especially on a weekend. They weren't going too far, just up a ways, well into the massive rock formations along the trail. Jemimah was going to commit suicide. What more fitting a place to die than in the Garden of the Gods?

"Move," Brenda screamed at Jemimah.

"Where are we going?" Although Jemimah had lived there for some time, she hadn't yet ventured out on the trails running parallel to the highway.

"Don't worry about that. You keep moving." Brenda waved the gun at her. "And don't think you can get away. I have no problem with shooting you in the back."

"Why did you kill Charlie, Brenda?" Jemimah said. "I thought you loved him."

"Charlie was a loser. He was incapable of love. He was like a bee, flitting from flower to flower."

"What were you wishing for, Brenda? Maybe a family? To be like your mother?"

"Keep my mother out of this. I hated that bitch. She couldn't keep a man happy. Hey, I know what you're doing. Don't try to psychoanalyze me. I've been with the best of them."

"I know. Dr. Garland in Denver," Jemimah said.

"Keep walking, you nosy bitch. I'll tell you when to stop," Brenda poked the pistol into Jemimah's back.

A mile farther across the low mountainous terrain, they stopped in front of Devil's Throne, an overhang that stretched over a shallow cave like a huge awning. The walls of the cave were painted in solid dark colors, with Wiccan and anarchy symbols throughout in white and bright red. It resembled a huge mythic altar where maidens were brought to be sacrificed to the gods. Jemimah felt a tinge of terror run through her veins. How could such a dark, ill-omened place exist in the center of so much beauty?

Brenda pushed her toward the back of the overhang. Crude rock-hewn steps wound their way to the top. It was a difficult climb, Brenda constantly poking at her spine with the pistol. Jemimah feared she would become more irritated and just shoot her on the spot. When they finally made it to the top, Jemimah saw a makeshift table made from a long flat rock just ahead. Next to the table was a grotesque assemblage of animal skulls, fur and feathers atop a long wooden pole balanced precariously in its brace. Jemimah assumed the scepter pertained to an ancient occult god worshipped in secret ceremonies held in this huge alcove. Brenda broke into the silence of her thoughts.

"Well, Miss Investigator, this is where you get off. Speak your last request, your prayers for your fellow man, world peace or whatever it is you people pray for. Then you're going to jump off the edge there, a fitting finale to this drama." Brenda's hand swept dramatically across the horizon.

"You can't get away with this, Brenda. Let me help you out. I can arrange for you to spend time in treatment."

"I'm not crazy. No way. You want to put me in a mental institution. As soon as I'm done with you, I'll be taking off. Nobody will ever find me. Now shut up and move." Brenda continued to jab her back with the weapon.

"What's this going to accomplish, Brenda, killing one more person?"

"Can't be any worse punishment for one or five." Brenda looked at her with disgust. "Move. Just a few more feet. By this time tomorrow you'll be just another headline in the newspaper."

Brenda prodded her toward the edge with the barrel of the gun. As they walked past the table, Jemimah suddenly turned and grabbed the wooden scepter. She swung it like a bat at Brenda, knocking her off balance, then scurried down the rocks as the woman scrambled to her feet. She didn't look back as she ran toward home. To her relief, Brenda was nowhere in sight. She quickened her pace. Her heart skipped a beat as she heard the definite ping of a bullet ricocheting off a rock.

Brenda fired wildly, emptying the magazine. She threw the gun down and screamed obscenities. Jemimah could see her ranch up ahead. She knew she might not be able to make it all the way into the house to retrieve her gun and her phone. Out of breath, she crouched behind the small shed attached to the barn. The only visible weapons were a shovel, a pitchfork and a hoe. She knew none of them would be effective against a gun, but she had a feeling Brenda was out of ammo and infinitely more comfortable with a knife. She reached for the shovel, gripping it firmly as she worked her way carefully toward the house.

Jemimah didn't hear the footsteps as Brenda snuck in behind her. She turned as Brenda raised her arm, clutching the knife, and grabbed her around the neck. Brenda's strength was fueled by hostility and anger. She pulled Jemimah around like she was a Raggedy Ann doll. Jemimah struggled to pull herself free.

The next ten minutes were a blur. The growling snarl of Jemimah's dog echoed as she sailed through the air, firmly entrenching her teeth around Brenda's arm. Brenda screamed. The knife dropped to the floor. Molly's vice-like jaws held Brenda firmly on the ground. "Get her off me," Brenda screamed.

The shrill sound of sirens broke around them. Detective Romero and Tim McCabe drove into the driveway and jumped out of the cruiser, pistols drawn. McCabe seized Brenda and held her down as Romero cuffed her and pushed her into the backseat of the vehicle. Jemimah took a deep breath and leaned on the shovel as Rick walked toward her.

"Damn," he said. "Are you all right?"

"I am now," she said, bending down to shower her dog with kisses.

52

Lieutenant Romero stood next to Jemimah at the memorial held for the four murdered women. Even for the month of August, the temperature was unbearably hot, although the sky was dark and overcast. The church was filled to capacity with mourners and the curious. Jemimah felt comfortable with her shoulder leaning against Rick. Whitney showed up and took a seat on the other side of her. She could feel Rick stiffen up.

Friends, neighbors and relatives occupied the polished wooden pews of St. Francis Cathedral. Photos of the victims adorned the small table on the altar, surrounded by an overabundance of freshly cut flowers. Still in the throes of grief, the families of the victims huddled together. The priest recited the final prayers and led the congregation outside through the church doors. Mourners piled into the waiting limos to make the lonely drive to the cemetery.

Once outside, a swarm of reporters waited. With microphones pointed at his face, Romero thanked his fellow officers for their help in solving the case and then handed the microphone over to Sheriff Bobby Medrano.

The arrest of Brenda Mason had been a slow and tedious process. Romero was impatient to put the lid on it. The evidence against her was overwhelming. Even the best defense attorney would have a hard time getting her anything but a life sentence. Not only did Forensics find her bloody print on the cigarette lighter in Charlie's SUV, but strands of her hair were mixed with the blood on his shirt. Her hair was also present on some of the victims' clothing. Her DNA and more hair were found on the murder weapon, and the jewelry of one of the victims was discovered in the glove box of her car.

* * *

Brenda was not at all comfortable in her jail cell at the Santa Fe County Adult Detention Center, a building she had driven by hundreds of times and where she had on occasion visited incarcerated friends. To top it off, her roommate Sonja Swentzel refused her phone calls so that she couldn't even ask her to bring some of her personal belongings to the jail. After all she had done for that bitch. She had half a mind to turn her in to the State for embezzling.

53

Sitting at a long table in the interrogation room the following day, Brenda was unsmiling, nervous, and struggling to maintain her self-assurance. She needed a hit of something, anything. A female deputy stood a few feet away near the door. Jemimah sat on the other side of the two-way mirror. Brenda leaned forward on the edge of her chair.

"Can I have a cigarette?" she asked Detective Romero.

Romero tossed her his package and extended his lighter. "Sure."

"So why am I here? Some traffic thing or something?" she smiled broadly, her eyes wide.

Romero reminded her that she had been arrested for the murder of Charlie Cooper and the attempted murder of Jemimah Hodge.

"Murder? I thought Charlie shot himself somewhere out in the boonies. And who is this Jemimah Hodge person?" she said.

"Miss Mason, let me ask the questions. Tell me what you were doing on the afternoon of July 26," Romero said.

"That was over a month ago. Ask me what I was doing yesterday," she laughed.

Romero took a deep breath and repeated the question.

"Give me an idea of what you did the week before you heard about Charlie's death," he said.

"Listen, I left Santa Fe about a week before Charlie offed himself. Went to Las Vegas. Spent a little time vegging out in front of a slot machine and then flew back," she said, taking a deep drag on her cigarette.

"Where did you stay in Las Vegas?" Romero asked.

"Some flea-bag hotel on the strip. I didn't spend much time there." She crunched the cigarette butt into the ashtray.

By the time Brenda was ten, she could tell a big lie with a straight face.

Romero opened his briefcase, pulled out some photos, and laid them in front of Brenda. It was Charlie, lying in a pool of blood. For less than a second her body went stiff and she gripped the edges of the chair. She looked at Romero without emotion. He laid another batch of photos in front of her. These were of the bodies of the murdered women.

Her eyes widened. "Who are they?"

"These are the four women whose bodies were discovered at the Crawford Ranch," Romero said. "Do you know anything about them?"

"Did you get me a lawyer? I don't have anything to say," she said.

Romero looked at Detective Chacon.

"This is going nowhere, Brenda," Romero said. "It would be in your best interest to cooperate. Tell us what happened and I'll see if we can cut some kind of a deal with the DA."

"You mean in your best interest, don't you?" Brenda was belligerent. "I don't know anything about those women; I don't know anything about Charlie. Last time I saw him he was fine. Look, I know I'm entitled to a lawyer, so quit screwing me around."

The questioning continued for two hours. Brenda continued to throw up an invisible shield between her and the detectives. Jemimah Hodge had discussed Brenda's mental condition with him at length. He was beginning to believe it. Romero pulled some papers from his briefcase and began to read out loud:

"I snuck into the house through the downstairs sunroom, which was never locked. Charlie and the blonde were passed out on the bed. I lifted her off the bed and placed her in the little red wagon and wheeled it over to the barn. It wasn't hard to kill her. She wasn't moving anyway. I left the body on the tarp and dragged it down the ramp into the tunnel."

Brenda looked at the detective. She was stunned that he had her personal journal. Where had she left it? That fucking Sonja.

Right before their eyes Brenda went from calm and composed to agitated and combative. She ran to the door, screaming. The deputies tried to subdue her as she scratched and kicked, arms and legs flailing. They managed to pin her to the floor.

Brenda let out a blood-curdling scream that could be heard all the way down to the end of the corridor.

"Momma!"

54

Because the bodies had been discovered on prehistoric Indian ruins, Tim McCabe felt compelled to meet with the elders of nearby pueblos in order to facilitate a cleansing. On the first of August, he traveled to each of the pueblos to arrange for a time they could gather at the ruins. Elders at Cochiti, San Felipe, Santa Ana and Sandia pueblos agreed to a mutual time to visit San Lazaro for the ceremony.

Although the murders had occurred on the ranch and not on the ruins, who was to say that the ranch at one time hadn't been part of the original sacred pueblo ground? The murders were a spiritual contaminant and although no members of the Tano tribes existed at the present time, some area tribes probably originated from these early inhabitants. Saint Lazarus, the namesake of the pueblo, was a man who had been raised from the dead during biblical times. It was fitting that the ruins should be returned to their original state.

For the cleansing ceremony, McCabe saw the need to choose the feast day of another saint, because St. Lazarus was not one whose feast was celebrated by the Native American pueblos. He chose August 10, a feast day celebrated by the Picuris Pueblo to honor their patron saint, San Lorenzo, or Saint Lawrence. San Lorenzo was a deacon who had been sentenced to die on a metal grate over a roaring fire. While being grilled to death, he had exhibited great strength and courage. In addition, on the evening of his feast day, a meteor shower known as the burning tears of St. Lawrence had been seen in the sky.

At sundown, McCabe and the four elders stood in the center of the property holding bowls of white cornmeal and small bundles of freshly picked sage. The shaman offered a pinch of pollen to the setting sun and then walked to the four corners of the ruins, chanting a prayer at each. On that day the sky had been a deep cerulean blue, with fragments of swollen white clouds drifting above them. The sun was spreading the last of its light. The natural spring below Medicine Rock erupted through the ground, its crystal waters forming a deep pool. It was a good day for a cleansing ceremony; a good day for a new beginning.

Epilogue

United Airlines flight 782 departed from Albuquerque International Airport at 7:23 a.m. on the morning of December 23. It arrived at Brasilia, the capitol of Brazil, at 4:30 the next afternoon. It was Christmas Eve, the middle of winter in New Mexico, but here it was the middle of summer. The woman could see the beach from her window seat as the plane taxied in to park. Bikini-clad females and muscle-bound men pursued their tans on bright beach towels.

It had been an uneventful flight. The passengers reached for their belongings and prepared to disembark from the A-380 jumbo airliner. Sonja Swentzel smoothed the slight wrinkles on her Anna Sui silk suit and leaned down to adjust the strap on her Christian Louboutin platform pumps. As she neared the exit ramp, she placed the Gucci sunglasses square on her face and held on tight to her shoulder bag.

CPSIA information can be obtained at www.ICGtesting.com
Printed in the USA
244793LV00008B/141/P